Allie Stuart Povall is a native Mississippian and a Vietnam veteran. He holds degrees from the University of Mississippi and Yale Law School. Povall served two combat tours during the Vietnam War, one as the executive officer of the USS St. Francis River, a rocket ship providing close-in fire support to troops ashore and in support of swift boat operations. This is his sixth book.

In loving memory of Francis Earl Neir III, my shipmate and my brother, who brought joy into my life and the lives of many.

Allie Stuart Povall

THE THINGS HE LOST THERE

A Story of the Vietnam War

Austin Macauley Publishers
LONDON · CAMBRIDGE · NEW YORK · SHARJAH

Copyright © Allie Stuart Povall 2024

All rights reserved. No part of this publication may be reproduced, distributed, or transmitted in any form or by any means, including photocopying, recording, or other electronic or mechanical methods, without the prior written permission of the publisher, except in the case of brief quotations embodied in critical reviews and certain other non-commercial uses permitted by copyright law. For permission requests, write to the publisher.

Any person who commits any unauthorized act in relation to this publication may be liable to criminal prosecution and civil claims for damages.

This is a work of fiction. Names, characters, businesses, places, events, locales, and incidents are either the products of the author's imagination or used in a fictitious manner. Any resemblance to actual persons, living or dead, or actual events is purely coincidental.

Ordering Information
Quantity sales: Special discounts are available on quantity purchases by corporations, associations, and others. For details, contact the publisher at the address below.

Publisher's Cataloging-in-Publication data
Povall, Allie Stuart
The Things He Lost There

ISBN 9798891558038 (Paperback)
ISBN 9798891558045 (Hardback)
ISBN 9798891558052 (ePub e-book)

Library of Congress Control Number: 2024914320

www.austinmacauley.com/us

First Published 2024
Austin Macauley Publishers LLC
40 Wall Street, 33rd Floor, Suite 3302
New York, NY 10005
USA

mail-usa@austinmacauley.com
+1 (646) 5125767

I acknowledge with gratitude the editorial assistance provided by my loving wife, Janet Povall.

Table of Contents

Prologue	15
Prelude Tet	16
Chapter One: Chapel Hill	18
Chapter Two: The California Coast	25
Melanie	27
Chapter Three: The Ship	30
The Black River	36
Melanie	42
Chapter Four: The First Cruise	43
Chapter Five: Cam Ranh Bay	49
Phu Quoc	52
Rock Jaw	58
The Pueblo	60
Chapter Six: Subic Bay	62
Tet	66
A Letter from Melanie	71
Chapter Seven: Hong Kong	73
Melanie	75
Chapter Eight: Yokosuka	76
The Yokosuka Officers' Club Junior Officers' Dance	79

Cohen	*81*
Another Letter from Melanie	*82*
The Admiral's Daughter	*83*
Dinner with the Chiefs	*85*
Chapter Nine: The Second Cruise	**88**
The Tokyo Expressway	*89*
Yokosuka	*101*
The Letter to Melanie	*104*
Underway Training	*107*
Chapter Ten: The Third Cruise	**119**
August 1, 1968	*119*
Cam Ranh Bay	*121*
Tacloban	*122*
Melanie	*124*
The Tacloban Death March	*125*
Melanie	*128*
Chapter Eleven: Back to the Gunline	**130**
Melanie	*134*
Chapter Twelve: The Investigation	**135**
Melanie	*136*
Report of the Investigation	*137*
Subic Bay	*142*
Melanie	*143*
Chapter Thirteen: The Taiwan Straits	**145**
February 1969	*145*
Chapter Fourteen: Melanie	**159**
August 15, 1969	*159*

Chapter Fifteen: Chapel Hill   **161**
   October 1969   *161*
Chapter Sixteen: Requiem   **168**
   October 1984   *168*

A stone, a leaf, an unfound door; of a stone, a leaf, a door and all of the forgotten faces.

* * *

O waste of loss, in the hot mazes, lost, among bright stars on this most weary unbright cinder, lost! Remembering speechlessly we seek the great forgotten language, the lost lane-end into heaven, a stone, a leaf, an unfound door. Where? When?

– Thomas Wolfe, *Look Homeward Angel*.

Prologue

They were always there, and they were always evocative, even after fifteen years and another season of his life. The sound of a single small airplane, high overhead, its drone reverberating off the earth below. A helicopter, coming up fast and hard over a tree line. A cat-eyed girl with straight brown hair, parted on the left, neck-length, the sweep of it across her forehead captured by a gold barrette on the side opposite the parting. Fireworks, illuminating the sky like trip-wire flares or five-inch rockets arching toward a target. A lone jet fighter high overhead, its thin white contrail cutting across an indigo sky, its sound, like his life, broken by distance and time. And the others: a 1960s vintage sports car—an MGB or a Triumph or an Austin Healey. Cigarette smoke carried on a wafting breeze. Coffee at daybreak. The first stars and the crepuscular light of morning and evening twilight. Venus, low on the western horizon. A full moon rising across quiet green water. A gray foaming sea, angry, roiled by the wind.

These images evoked for him a time in his life that marked the end of everything he had known before it, everything he had been before it, and everything he had hoped to become but wouldn't. For until that precise moment when his world imploded with savage suddenness, his life had been an easy continuum, a sweet trajectory that, in spite of hiccups and bounces, moved him inexorably along the path from childhood to adulthood, from promise to fulfillment of promise.

All of that ended with one decision that he made, and what he surrendered then he was not able, and would never be able, to reclaim: the cat-eyed girl, joy, laughter, his youth, love, optimism. He would grieve the losses the rest of his life, for once forfeited, those things could not be reclaimed. They were lost forever. They were the things he lost there.

Prelude
Tet

He crouched behind the steel bulkheads of the ship's bridge. The captain was there, sitting, too, and across the bridge a quartermaster lay dead, his head blown open by a machine-gun bullet. Machine-gunfire tore into the little ship as she rotated to bring her rocket launchers to bear on the North Vietnamese machine-gun emplacements along the Perfume River at a city called Hue. Jack, the executive officer and navigator, took a steel shard from the bridge bulkhead in his arm. Liam McNamara, the weapons officer sat in a corner, wounded in the shoulder, losing blood by the second.

Jesus, Jack thought. *How the hell did I get here? I mean, two months ago I was in Chapel Hill going to classes and being with Melanie. And now, this? How in Jesus' name did I get myself into this situation? I may not survive this. In fact, I don't think I will. I think we're going to take a recoilless rifle shell into the side and it'll set off the rockets we carry and all there'll be left of the USS Black River will be a cloud of smoke and a memory. God. What a way to go.*

He crawled over and found the sound-powered phone operator, as machine-gun bullets tore into the Black River's sides. The air was thick with shrapnel, and he took the phone from the dead sailor and called below, "Wallis, get the corpsman up here. Both the captain and Mr. McNamara are wounded. And tell the starboard-side rocket launchers to stand by. When we get aligned with the shore, we are going to open up. Got it?"

"Yessir, XO. We're standing by."

Jack crawled to the captain, barely conscious. He had taken shrapnel in his leg and was bleeding heavily. "Hold on, Captain. Help's on the way. I'm going to open up with the starboard-side launchers in just a second and we'll suppress this machine-gunfire. Hang on."

Captain Stockwell gave him a thumbs-up, and Jack stood and watched as the Black completed her rotation, and he ordered all engines stopped and told the Combat Information Center to open fire. Then the rocket launchers came to life, and mark nine rockets began eating the shoreline. The machine-gun fire stopped as the shore erupted in a conflagration of fire and explosions.

The corpsman, Chief Petty Officer Ortiz, appeared. "Jesus god," he said as he surveyed the disaster on the bridge.

"Start with Mr. McNamara, Chief Ortiz. I'm going to turn this thing around and get the hell out of here."

He began another turn, and this time there was no fire from the shore. It was gone, eaten by the Black's rockets. *Christ almighty*, he thought. *What the fuck am I doing here? How did this happen? How did I put myself into the middle of this holocaust? Jesus. This duty station was supposed to be a can of corn. Home-ported in Yokosuka, Japan. Japanese girls. Navy nurses. The Officers' Club. It was supposed to be a piece of cake. This isn't what I signed on for. How did it happen this way? How?*

Chapter One
Chapel Hill

Autumn had come early that year to the Carolina piedmont. The days were golden, the afternoons luminous with waning sunlight, and everywhere there was the smell of burning leaves, suffused with the faint cologne of nostalgia, which overhung that beautiful old place like the wood smoke that pooled over the town in the evenings, when people got home and started fires in their fireplaces.

Jack Houston was in school again—graduate school—after three years as a naval officer. Several thousand miles away, the war in Vietnam raged toward its apogee, or maybe its nadir, and each day seemed to bring reports of new disasters, of more deaths. But the war was in his past now, and he had shucked his officer's uniforms for Levis, flannel shirts, his old Navy foul-weather jacket and the Boondockers he had worn at Naval OCS.

Each morning, he sat in the sunny UNC quadrangle before his first class, drinking coffee and smoking a Marlboro as he read the Durham morning newspaper. Around him was the patina of time: old brick buildings, musty and moldy, and old trees, their leaves colored and some already brittle. Hundreds of students milled about the quad and made their way to class. Coeds in Villager outfits and hard-soled Pappagallo shoes click-clacked across the old bricks. Fraternity boys in light blue Gant shirts and starched khaki pants, in Weejuns and Gold Cup socks, sauntered confidently to their first classes.

He didn't know it then—*couldn't* know it then—but the war in Vietnam wasn't over for him, even though he had spent some eighteen months cruising off the Vietnam coast on the USS Princeton, an amphibious assault ship. That ship's mission had been to put Marine Battalion Landing Teams ashore to fight the Vietcong and North Vietnamese regulars who operated with near impunity up and down the coast of South Vietnam. Their Marines had landed at Chu Lai and Danang and had participated in vicious operations with benign names like Barrel Roll, Jackstay, Cedar Falls, Junction City, Sea Swallow and Hastings. Jack had earned ribbons that he wore on Wednesday nights to Navy Reserve meetings in Raleigh, but the next day he would be back in the clothes he wore to school, clothes that symbolized his independence from the rigidity and iron discipline of a Navy ship. His clothes were standard attire for a graduate student, just as the preppy uniforms that the Greek undergraduates wore were standard for them.

Jack had found girls at Carolina. Scores of them. But he had settled on Melanie Lawton, a beautiful young Charleston, West Virginia woman with thick brown hair and clear blue cat-eyes and a beautiful, lithe, athlete's body. In November, he took her in his MGB to Charlottesville for 'Openings', a weekend of parties at the center of which was the Carolina-Virginia game, which Virginia won handily. They stayed with another Navy veteran who had served with him on the Princeton and who had then returned to graduate school in the UVA MBA program.

It was in late November, and the days in Charlottesville were suffused with golden sunlight that strained to penetrate the ubiquitous smoke from burning leaves and was softened by the angle of the sun itself, low now in the southern sky. Melancholia was heavy in the Virginia autumn air. Cold weather and a dreary eastern winter were not far away.

Sitting in front of a UVA fraternity house, he had a strong sensation that he was not supposed to be there, or be in graduate school at Carolina. He was overwhelmed with the sense that he had moved on, that he was no longer the soft, disorganized undergraduate who loved history and class, fraternity parties and Ivy League clothes. As he sat there watching the UVA fraternity boys party on that golden Sunday afternoon, he felt that he wanted more from life than what academia offered, but it was as though he had made an irrevocable decision, and he did not know how to find his way into the outside world—the world beyond the Navy and the cloistered temples of academia. As he sat there, he wondered whether he could even *make it* on the outside. Maybe he was a misfit, doomed to either a military or an academic career. Maybe he had made a mistake in choosing graduate school. Maybe he belonged in law school. But he had no money for it. He had no money for anything. He was tottering on the razor's edge of penury, and it scared him. What then?

Upon Jack's return to Chapel Hill from Virginia, he opened a letter from BUPERS, the Navy Bureau of Personnel, in Washington. 'The Letter', as he would come to call it, was written by a 'detailer', a naval officer who made officer assignments. In it, the detailer invited him back into the Navy, setting forth a powerful and persuasive argument: you were a high performer and a high achiever and the kind of officer the Navy needs and wants. And maybe, if you think about it, the Navy had, and has, what you were looking for: an opportunity to lead men, a sense of belonging, excitement, and reward. Come back, the detailer said, come back and be a member of the Navy team.

The timing of the letter couldn't have been better from the Navy's standpoint: Jack indeed was on the ragged edge of financial ruin, and his economic insecurity was high. He was unhappy with the student's life, and he felt that he had actually lost ground in the transition from naval officer—from leading men and driving a ship and taking responsibility not only for his own actions, but for the actions of others—to graduate student. Jack had tried to go back to college, but the boy who had loved that world was gone, replaced by a man trying to live in a boy's world. So, he spent many of his evenings drinking—alone. He knew that it was not a good thing, but it allowed him to escape the life he had in Chapel Hill and to dream of his golden California days, driving his MGB with the top down and sleeping with beautiful tan California girls and Midwestern girls who had come to California to catch a naval officer for marriage.

He was sorely tempted by the letter, but he wondered about going back in, about people saying that he couldn't make it on the outside, that he was a failure, a loser. At that point in his life, what people thought and said was paramount. He had no other measuring stick, no other standard to guide him. His father, his polar star, was dead, and in the aftermath of his death, Jack's grieving mother was emotionally unavailable to him. He was adrift, alone, lost. Along with many of his fellow Princeton junior officer friends, he had always thought that many careers naval officers were losers. And the biggest losers of all were those who had gotten out of the Navy and then returned to the service. They were the ones who couldn't 'make it' on the 'outside' and had come back into the service to survive. And now, it occurred to him that he might be one, too. *I can't leave Carolina*, he concluded. *Not now. I must go on and at least finish out the year. Then decide. Decide about graduate school, about Melanie, about the Navy.*

Melanie? He loved her more than anything in the world. She was everything he had ever thought of finding or having: pretty, intelligent, and cultured. Good breeding, they would say in Mississippi, his home. You couldn't beat good breeding, his mother always said. It was reflected in everything from table manners to the size of various body parts: small hands, feet, ankles and bones in general, but thankfully, not boobs. He was a neck and a boob man, and Melanie had those, along with his mother's other marks of good breeding.

And then the paradigm-busting explosion occurred. It was the Wednesday after his trip to Charlottesville and the day before Thanksgiving. Jack was in a classroom awaiting the start of a European History class, and he was talking to a girl. Nothing special, nothing harmful or threatening or out of the ordinary. Just a routine pre-class conversation. The professor, a tall, gaunt relic of a man in a baggy gray suit, entered the classroom, and the class quieted. He took his place at the lectern, adjusted his wire-rimmed glasses, and then exploded. "Get out," he screamed in Jack's general direction. "Get out of this class. I'm sick of your talking. Now get out."

The class quickly became as quiet as death. Jack swallowed hard. The professor was looking directly into his eyes. But Jack did nothing. After all, he was twenty-five years old. He was a veteran. He was a *man*. This was grade-school stuff. The professor wouldn't do this to *him*. *Couldn't* do this to Jack Houston, a grown man, a Vietnam veteran. The professor had to know that he was a real grownup. It must be directed at someone behind Jack, or in front of him, but certainly not him.

The professor left the lectern and stormed down the side aisle of the classroom, now pointing directly at Jack. The ancient specter was beside himself. "Get out," he screamed. "You and you. I've had it with you two," he screamed. "Now out!" His face was red and twisted with anger. Embarrassment rolled through the class like a bad smell, and students with twisted faces turned to look at Jack, knowing what Jack was denying: that he was the grade-school miscreant.

Jack wrinkled his forehead in disbelief and pointed incredulously at his chest. Horror and shame spread across his face that this could be happening to someone his age, to someone of his stature. "Yes, you," the professor screamed. "Out. And you too," he bellowed at the girl next to him. "You get out too. I'm sick of it. Sick and tired of you two talking in this class." She was an undergraduate, but him? Surely not him?

Jack sat there stunned, like he had just been pole-axed. But he quickly decided that he wasn't going to take it. He was paying a lot of money to take this fossil's class. It was money hard-earned and saved out of combat pay, just for this opportunity. He would tell him that, tell him that he was paying the professor good, precious dollars to teach, so get your skinny academician's ass back up there and do it. He wouldn't leave this class with his tail tucked between his legs. He was a naval officer, and he was twenty-five years old, and by God no skinny piece of academic shit was going to run him out of class like some damn tenth-grade cutup.

And then, strangely, he felt himself rising. The old feeling had returned, the feeling that somehow, he must deserve this. It was a feeling that had haunted him from childhood. His grade school teachers had instilled it: he was unworthy. He was *bad*. And when challenged, especially by authority figures, his guilt for *being bad* made him simply cave in. It was a pattern that they had established early in his life and that had exerted its strange dominance over him ever since with one exception: his time in the Navy. So, he got up and skulked out, still not believing that it was happening but unwilling to take on the authority figure. He just wanted it to be over, and leaving was the quickest way to make it be over.

The other 35 or so students in the class watched him go, as embarrassed perhaps as he was, even though they didn't know who or how old he was or what he had been, or done, before graduate school. Jack *did* know, however, and he knew one other thing: he was through. He could never go back to that class, or any other class. He had lost everything: his pride, his desire to be a student, his sense of self-worth—always tenuous—and his purpose for being in Chapel Hill.

That night, he drove to Melanie's apartment. She greeted him at the door.

"Did you hear what happened to me today?"

"Yes, I did. It's all over graduate school. Unbelievable."

"Absolutely unbelievable," he said. "I feel like shit."

"Well, I wouldn't let it bother me. Go to see the professor and go back to class after Thanksgiving. Everyone will have forgotten. It'll be yesterday's news."

"It won't be yesterday's news for me. It'll be today's news from now on. I can't go back. I'd be too embarrassed. I mean, I'm twenty-five years old and I got thrown out of class like some high school sophomore. I just can't believe that it happened to me. Just can't believe it."

He shook his head lugubriously and stared, as though trying to comprehend the classroom catastrophe that had just fallen on him like a five-inch shell. "Look," she said. "So, it hurts. I understand. But I promise you no one else around here gives a damn. They're all narcissistic and so focused on themselves and grades that they couldn't care less about your pain. Just put it behind you and go on. I sure as hell don't care."

"Let me tell you something else," he said. "I got a letter from the Navy inviting me to come back in. I'm seriously considering it."

She looked at him, incredulity now in *her* eyes. "You're *not,* are you?"

"Yes."

"Why? Because of this? Jesus, don't do this when this wound is still fresh. Give it a few days. Or weeks. Please."

He was silent.

"I understand how you feel," she said. "Or I think I do. You're hurting. And I understand that. But don't make such a huge decision while this wound is still fresh. Just wait. Please." She took his arm and tugged gently. "Please."

He stood. "Come on," he said. "Let's go get something to eat. How about the Rathskeller?"

"Okay, but I…I'm concerned about you, Jack. I really am. I think you're about to make a big mistake. You always said if you didn't like graduate school you would go to law school. Well, do it. You can get in. And you'll do well. You're smart and you write beautifully. Please don't go back in the Navy. You're too intelligent for that."

"I don't have the money to go to law school," he said, "and I don't know how to get any, except by doing the only thing I know how to do: be a naval officer." And he didn't. He was done, and he knew it. All that was left for him was for Melanie to know that he was done, and after dinner that night, she, too, knew that his great academic experiment was over.

And so, on a gray day at the end of November 1967, he awakened in his trailer and called the Navy detailer and told him he was ready to go. Three days later, he had orders to a ship home-ported in Yokosuka, Japan, and a mover came and packed up his few things for shipment to his duty station. Then, he loaded his MGB with clothes and uniforms, aimed it west and headed for California, with its golden beaches and golden girls and the halcyon times of only a year before. And in his rear-view mirror, he watched Chapel Hill and all that it had symbolized—a safe, non-threatening career in the ivy-covered, cloistered halls of higher education—disappear in a cloud of shame and razor-sharp humiliation.

He climbed the eastern mountain range and began the long gradual descent into America's heartland and headed west on a journey that would quickly take him from the Carolina autumn and return him to that place where he had found what he thought was manhood. He did not turn south toward home, in Mississippi. His mother was preoccupied with her daughter, who had moved to Nashville upon her graduation from Ole Miss. There was nothing at home for him anymore. It was time to move on. And he did. West toward California.

Chapter Two
The California Coast

Jack's duty station was to be executive officer—number two in the chain of command—on the USS Black River, a small rocket ship home-ported—at least, theoretically he would learn to his regret—in Yokosuka, Japan. He was thrilled with the billet. His cousin had been stationed in Yokosuka, and Jack had enjoyed visiting him there when he had passed through on the Princeton. The Navy base had a large expatriate community, close-knit, like a small town, and they drank together and danced together and dined together and supported each other. But his cousin was gone, so this was going to be different; now Jack was alone. He would no longer have his cousin or his Princeton buddies, no longer have the place he had carved out for himself on the Princeton, where he was surrounded by friends and mentors. And he didn't know it then, but what he was headed for was not the Princeton, with its cozy, close-knit wardroom, spacious staterooms, and restaurant-quality food. What he was headed for now was to be unlike anything he had known—had ever experienced—in the Navy the first time around.

As he drove into the western sun, he wondered about his decision. Wondered about leaving everything he had loved—all the freedom of civilian life—for the things he had hated about the Navy: loneliness, boredom, isolation, the tedium of long days and nights at sea punctuated by terror: bridge watches and driving the ship in formation. Those bridge watches had left him unable to sleep, nervous, irritable, dreading the next watch. And now, here he was going back to it, but this time, he was going back into it in spades. As executive officer, he would be responsible for navigation, for gunfire control, and for the overall administration of the ship and for executing the captain's orders, all things he had never done. It would be the Princeton multiplied by about five. But he needed money, and this seemed the easiest, quickest way to get it. A lot of it. He also needed training before reporting to his ship, and the

Navy had graciously ordered it, so he headed west for Treasure Island, in the heart of San Francisco Bay.

He had very little money left after his near-semester-long stay at Carolina, barely enough to get him across country, so he ate cheaply and drank coffee so he could drive around the clock to avoid motel fees. Sometimes at night, he would pull to the side of the road and put his seat back, cover himself with an old Navy blanket he had stolen off the Princeton, and sleep long enough to allow him to shove off again. He drove across the monochromatic Kansas grain factory, flat and somnolent as winter approached, driving ninety miles an hour while America's sleeping heartland rolled past him, all of it an equable buckskin color.

The radio music there was the same as what he had been listening to in Carolina, minus the Carolina beach music: 'Ode to Billie Joe', 'To Sir with Love', 'Wendy', 'I'm a Believer', 'Light my Fire', by the Doors, 'Groovin'', and Aretha Franklin demanding respect. The MGB pulled up the long, gradual rise to Denver, where he spent a night with an old Princeton friend, who questioned him about his decision to return to the Navy and tried to discourage him. "You can get a job here. I promise. A good job paying you a lot of money. Companies around here are begging for college graduates. Shitcan this idea of going back in the Navy. Call 'em and tell 'em no, that you're staying here. You can stay with me until you get situated. Please."

"No, Fred. I've made a commitment and I'm going to keep it. Besides, all of my stuff has already been shipped out there. So, I've got to go."

The next day, Jack borrowed fifty bucks, and then headed northwest across Utah and Nevada and on into San Francisco and his return to the fleet. As the bright pastel city approached, he began to wonder again: *What in god's name are you doing? This feeling that you can recapture the joy of the young junior officers of the Princeton wardroom is an illusion. They, and that time, are gone. Gone like your money. Gone like your father. Gone like your dreams of graduate school and a teaching sinecure. And what you will find in Japan is anyone's guess. What have you done? Abort! Abort! Go home.*

It was too late. He was there, he had orders, and he had no money to get home. He had come too far. It was a commitment, and men didn't make commitments and then break them. This obligation was for two years. Hell, he could hold his breath for two years, especially in Japan, the land of cameras, stereos, cheap jewelry and Seiko watches. And after two years he would have money, and he could go to law school. *Accept it,* the voice said. *It's time to accept your decision and move on.*

Melanie

She came at Christmas time, after he had completed his refresher training, and with him flush with Navy cash, they stayed at the St. Francis Hotel on Union Square. In the morning, they had Eggs Benedict, and at night they ate seafood and pasta and crusty loaves of bread on Fisherman's Wharf and drank cold California white wine. He bought champagne for the room, and they drank it and smoked cigarettes and made love. Afterward, she stood in her panties at the window, looking down on the bright Christmas lights around Union Square.

"Jack," she said gravely, "am I just a sex object for you?"

He was startled. "I don't know what that means," he said.

"It means that I'm really not a human being to you. Really not a person. Means you've objectified me and I'm just an object with which to make love. Have sex. Screw. Whatever you want to call it."

"No. Oh god no. I love you, Melanie. I love you more than anything in the world. I don't know what I can say stronger than that. I really do. That's why I wanted you to come out here."

"Well, the problem with that is that there are ways you show someone that you love them and frankly, I haven't seen many out of you. And really, you haven't acted any differently since I've known you. We go out. We have drinks. We dine. We go somewhere. We go to bed." She paused. "There's got to be more to a relationship than that. A relationship, to be real and fulfilling, at least for me, has got to have more direction than this. More purpose. More substance." She raised her hands and waved as though a supplicant to the world beyond the window. Then she pulled them in to her chest and turned to face him. Tears streaked her face.

He went to her. He held her close and stroked her hair. She tucked her face into his neck and cried softly, then pulled away. "I want more than this," she said. "Frankly, Jack, I didn't come out here just for this. This is just more of the same."

"I don't understand. What more? What did you come out here looking for?"

She was silent.

"An engagement?" he asked. "Marriage?"

She pulled away and looked out the window. "This was a big gamble for me," she said. "Coming all the way out here for Christmas. My mother warned me against it. She said if I came out here and you didn't ask me to marry you, then where would I be? And now here we are. Nothing's changed. So where am I?" She paused and looked him in the eyes. "Nowhere," she said. "No damn where."

He had feared this. He didn't want to marry. Too much uncertainty lay before him. Maybe he would get out to Westpac and decide it was she he wanted. Maybe he would want to fly her out to Japan and marry her there. Maybe they would spend time seeing the Japanese islands, visiting the old cities, mixing with other Navy couples in the Yokosuka Officers' Club. Maybe. But he couldn't be sure. "I can't ask you to marry me now," he said. "I don't know what's gonna happen out there. Let me get out to Japan and see if we can swing it. Let me see what's involved in bringing you out. It doesn't make sense to get married before we know that. It wouldn't be fair to you. I want you. I promise. Just be patient."

"Well, I certainly know how to do that, don't I? And fair to *me*? That's a joke, isn't it? Aren't we really talking about *you*? About what *you* want to do?"

He held her tightly. "I'm sorry," he said. "But please give me a chance to get the lay of the land. To see what this ship is like. What I'm gonna be doing. I promise. If I can make it work, I will. Okay?"

She pushed away, still facing him. "What other choice do I have? I can't make you marry me and I wouldn't if I could. I think it's clear that if you wanted to marry me, you would. There's no good reason not to. Those are just excuses. The real problem is that you don't love me enough to do it now." She pulled away and moved back to the window. "And you're not going to do it. That much is clear. So, as my mother says, it's time for me to fold my hand and cut my losses and go home."

"Come on now. Don't be that way." The words sounded hollow and condescending, and he knew it. He tried to change his tone. "We can work it out. I promise," he said softly. He approached her from behind and tried to turn her back to him. She jerked away.

"Just get your stuff and go," she said angrily, her back still to him. "I'm going to call and see if I can get an earlier flight back home. Today if possible."

He stood silently, perhaps because he did not know what else to say, perhaps because he knew that what she had said was true. But it was like that ignominious day in history class. He had been confronted, and rather than fight, he would simply move on. It was easier, and he probably *was* getting what he deserved. Finally, he spoke. "Okay," he said. "If that's the way you feel. I'll go. But I do love you and I hope you know that and I hope we can work it out where you can join me out there."

She wheeled to face him and said it with hardness, her voice laced with anger and venom: "You know Jack, you think you are so damn smooth with words. Like you can talk your way out of anything. Well, I'm sick of it. I don't want to hear you try to get out of the blame for this. This situation is not my doing. It's yours. So go put those smooth pretty words on someone else. But not on me. I've heard it all before. And I've just heard more of it today. And I've heard enough of it. So just get your stuff and go." There was fury in her words and voice now, so he did what he always did in situations like this: he withdrew. It was the professor's verbal assault all over again: *I must deserve this. I must be wrong. I must leave.* He was programmed that way and had been since an early age. So, he would go.

Outside, in the cold San Francisco wind, he caught a cab back to the base—his car was on its way to Yokosuka—and the Bachelor Officer Quarters. The base was deserted. It was Christmas Day, and he was alone. As alone as he had ever been. He sat in his room and smoked and wondered if he had made a mistake. And then he convinced himself that he had done the only thing he could do about Melanie: he must wait. Yes, he loved her, and yes, she was right, and no, she was not just a sex toy. *But I can't marry her now. That much I know because in two days I'm getting on a plane to Tokyo and a train down to Yokosuka and I'm catching my ship then. Maybe the ship will sit in Yokosuka Harbor and celebrate the New Year and everything will become clear to me. Maybe I will want her to come out and marry and when my tour is over, we can go back and I can go to law school. And maybe it won't become clear to me. But right now, I know that I just can't marry her. There are too many hurdles to clear for marriage at this time. I've just got to get out there and see. Just got to decide whether I can swing it now or whether I wait until this tour is over.*

Chapter Three
The Ship

She sat high in the water, rust running down her sides, looking for all the world like a small Japanese coastal freighter or a two-bit Chinese fishing scow. Her above-main deck structure, the 'superstructure'—a term that was joke on a ship like this one—arose out of the stern, and even the untrained eye could tell that her shape was a horrible design for heavy seas. There were eight rocket launchers on her deck, backed up with a five-inch gun. Smaller weapons—a couple of forty-millimeter pom-pom guns and two fifty-caliber machine guns bristled fore and aft and on the bridge. He guessed her length at about 200 feet. His heart sank. *We could have fitted five like her fore and aft on the Princeton's hangar deck, three abreast. What in the shit am I doing here? Surely there must have been an easier billet in which to make some money and get the hell out and go back to law school. Surely.* As the feeling of sickness gripped his stomach, his mind recalled a Bible verse from out of nowhere: *If God is for me, who or what can stand against me*? Or something like that. Jesus, he was in it now, and God, of whom he hadn't thought in years, had better be for him, because no one else on that garbage scow would. It was an old Navy tradition: hate the executive officer. The XO was always the bad cop to the CO's good cop. He would likely be hated by officers and enlisted men alike. It was just part of the job description.

    He returned to the BOQ and put on civilian clothes—a tan Harris tweed sport coat, brown wool slacks, a Gant tattersall plaid shirt, a bottle green club tie and British Walker wingtips—and then headed for the Officers' Club, which sat on the waterfront, a large two-story white masonry building that he remembered from previous stops in Yokosuka. It was cocktail time, and he was thirsty. The club had a large formal dining room up front, where a thin Japanese band warmed up with elevator music, but he headed to the rear of the old building to the Black Ships Bar, named to commemorate Commodore Perry's visit to these islands in 1853. There was already a sprinkling of officers present, drinking and smoking and playing various Navy dice games for drinks. The cigarette smoke pooled above the round game tables, and the men sank into crackling old leather club chairs. He sat at the bar and ordered his old cold-weather drink, a scotch and water. The gin gimlets and gin and tonics would await him in the tropics.

Some Navy nurses appeared, still in uniform, fresh off duty at the Naval Hospital. They took a table and ordered drinks. In the mirror, he could see a couple of them eyeing him and talking, and one of them caught his eye in the mirror and held his gaze and smiled. He got up and walked over. "Who are you?" she asked, "And what are you doing in a place like this? I've never seen you around here hanging out with this bunch of lifers."

"I'm Jack Houston," he replied. "And who are you?" She was cute, with brown hair that was teased and high on her head in the style of a year or two before. He liked Navy nurses, liked their uniforms and the way they fit them. Liked their hats—their 'covers', as the hats were called—and the way their covers sat on their heads.

She told him her name and introduced the others, who displayed varying degrees of interest. He was a one-nighter, they figured, so why waste time? These girls were looking for more. They were, like Melanie, looking for a relationship that would lead to someplace other than a bed.

His girl was Susan Geitner. She was from St. Louis, actually Kirkwood, a suburban town just west of the city. He knew about Kirkwood, because he had dated a girl from there early in his Princeton days: Judy Hoff. She was a great girl, but he had let her go, just as he had let so many of them go, always without explanation. He had just not been ready.

"You going to the dance tonight?" she asked.

"Don't know about the dance. I just got here from the States and came over for a drink and dinner. What's the dance deal?"

"It's Wednesday. They have a junior officers' dance here every Wednesday. It'll be next door in the Black Ships ballroom. Lots of people come. If you just got here, you can meet some people." She paused and sipped from her martini. "What brings you here anyway?"

"New duty station."

"Which one?"

"I'm to be executive officer of the Black River."

"What in god's name is the Black River? Sounds like the title of that Robert Mitchum movie."

"Yeah, I know. It does. But it's a rocket ship."

"And does a rocket ship shoot rockets?"

"Sometimes, I'm told. I hope it's not too often, though. I think I'd rather hang around here than shoot rockets on the Vietnam gunline."

"Well, good luck on that. Most of these ships stay in Vietnam more than they stay here. A lot more. Maybe yours will be the exception but if you shoot, you'll likely spend a lot of time shooting down there."

"I gather then that you had not heard of the Black River."

"No, but I do have a faint recollection that there were some rocket ships out there on the piers. But that's about all I know." She paused as if studying him. "Hmmmm. executive officer. That's a pretty good billet for someone as young as you. Where are you coming from?"

"I taught at Navy OCS. Before that I was on the Princeton, an amphibious assault ship."

He had lied, but it wasn't too big of a lie. He had gotten out the previous April after his tour on the Princeton and a year—an enticing year—teaching at OCS in Newport. It had been a glorious Newport summer of gorgeous sunny days and girls and concerts like the Newport Jazz Festival and the Newport Folk Festival and the America's Cup races, which the Intrepid had won. Then he had done those three months at Chapel Hill. He couldn't tell her that he had actually been discharged and been out for a few months. He was ashamed and didn't want her to know that he was a loser who couldn't make it on the outside and had to come back in to make a living.

"I know the Princeton. She's been through here a couple of times. Last one was just a few months ago. Maybe you were on it."

"No, I was at OCS teaching."

"How long were you at OCS?"

"Eighteen months," he lied. "Couple of years on the Princeton."

"Are you career? Sounds like you're staying in for life."

"I don't know about that. I thought I'd try this and if I like it, I may stay. Probably, I'll get out and go to law school when this one is over. I don't know. I haven't thought that far ahead."

"Well, this is quite a step up for you, isn't it?"

"Yeah, I guess. I don't know much about the job. But I assume that XO is a pretty good billet."

She took another sip on her martini.

"You dance?" she asked.

He smiled. "Yeah. You?"

"Yeah. Come on to the dance. You can show me what you got."

"I can show you what I got better somewhere other than the dance floor."

"You're bad," she said. "Bad. But I like that. Anyway, I'll take the dance floor. And then we can go from there. Okay?"

"That'll work for me," he said. Jack stood up. The others watched him. "Nice to meet you," he said, eschewing the regional collective pronoun 'y'all' for the more Navy-appropriate term 'you'. He turned away, and then turned back. "You want to have dinner with me?"

"Sure," she said. "That'd be nice."

They retired to the dining room. Outside, a cold drizzle had begun to fall, and steam from the old radiators along the walls covered the large paned windows with fog. On the sunset side of the dining room, the stained-glass windows were opaque with their colored glass, and a crowd had already gathered for dinner. The small Japanese band played 'My Way', and a Japanese singer belted out the song so that he sounded like a poor man's Frank Sinatra. Two couples danced in a desultory manner. Jack ordered another scotch and a martini for Susan Geitner.

"Did you grow up in Kirkwood?"

"Most of my life. We were in the Army for the first eight years, then Daddy retired to Kirkwood and I went to school there."

"Where'd you do nursing school?"

"In St. Louis at Barnes Hospital. I did two years at the University of Missouri first. You?"

"I'm an OCS guy. Did my undergraduate at Ole Miss."

"You say undergraduate. Did you go to graduate school."

"No," he lied again. The truthful answer to that question opened too many doors he didn't want to walk through with her.

"Then why'd you say undergraduate? That sounds like you're trying to make a distinction between undergraduate and graduate school."

"No. It's just that I may go to law school. I guess I was thinking of that."

"Well, what're you doing out here if you want to go to law school. Haven't you better be getting on with it?"

"Yeah, I guess. But I need some money to go and I figured this was a good opportunity to make some and save it."

"You could have borrowed the money. That's what my brother did. Borrowed every cent of it. Then you pay it back. That's a heck of a lot easier than coming way the hell out here and going into Joseph Conrad's heart of darkness, which is what Vietnam is. We see the results of that war. They come through here on their way back to the States and let me tell you, the results aren't pretty."

He studied her. She had deep brown eyes that reminded him of Alice Mossberg, a Jewish girl from Selma, Alabama, whom he had dated at Chapel Hill before he found Melanie. But Susan was more athletic-looking than Alice. Susan had a nice frame and long legs and a beautiful neck, with Alice's long eyelashes that tended to mask her dark eyes. He wondered how she would be in bed. He might be in love with Melanie, but Melanie had just given him a symbolic boot and besides, she was five or six thousand miles away.

They ordered dinner: him crabmeat au gratin, she a filet. He ordered a bottle of red wine and after dinner, a Drambuie with his coffee. She had coffee. No after-dinner drink.

"Do you always drink like this?" she asked.

"Like what?"

"Like having two or three drinks and two or three glasses of wine and now an after-dinner drink. You'd have to carry me out if I drank like that."

"I'd like to carry you out," he said.

She laughed. "Do you have a car?"

"I don't know. They are shipping it out but I don't know whether it's here yet. I'll have to check on it tomorrow."

"Let me see. I bet it's an Austin Healey 2000."

"I wish. No, but you're close. It's an MGB."

"Well, I was close, wasn't I?"

"Yeah. How'd you guess?"

"You just look like a British sports car guy. And I bet I can guess the color. Let's see." She put her chin in her hand and hummed. "Black. With a rag top."

"No, it's British racing green with a black leather top."

He drank the Drambuie. It warmed his stomach against the outside cold, which somehow seemed to have seeped into the large, high-ceilinged old room. The dining room had filled with couples having dinner and drinks before the dance. Even though it was billed as a junior officers' dance, Susan said that all ages and ranks attended and to watch out, some of these senior types had thin skins when they drank and would bristle if you even bumped into them.

"Screw 'em," he said. "They shouldn't even be there."

"Tough guy, huh? Well, we'll see when one of those captains kicks you across the dance floor."

He grinned. "He better have a big foot."

"He will," she said. "Don't worry about that. They all do."

Later, the band, a fine five-piece outfit, cranked up. They danced the boogaloo and shagged, then did a jerky variation of the twist. He held her tight when they slow-danced and she pushed her head into his shoulder and her face into his neck. She told him that he was the best slow-dancer she'd ever danced with, and he told her that she made him look good. "You are just too damn smooth," she said, and he held her tighter.

She went to the ladies' room, and a woman who had been watching them came over and asked him to dance. They slow-danced, and he could feel her large breasts pushing against him, and she took her legs and pressed them into his crotch, almost squeezing the breath out of him. Then there was a heavy hand on his shoulder. "That's enough," the deep-in-the-chest voice said. Jack turned. It was a fireplug of a man, stocky, broad, with a square head and a flat face that looked like a Boston terrier.

"Okay," Jack said. "She's all yours." The bulldog man eyed Jack suspiciously and said, "You damn right she is," and then yanked the woman off the floor. Jack returned to his table, where Susan awaited.

"I told you these guys could be rough, didn't I?"

"Yes, you did. Who the hell was that?"

"That, unbelievably, was the chaplain of the base staff. I don't know his name. I think it's either Byron or Brian or something like that. But he's in here all the time with her. They say she's hot to trot but you couldn't prove it by me. She is a hot dancer. I've seen her out there a number of times by herself, shaking it for everything she's got. One of these days she's going to entice some poor fool into believing he can get her into his bed and that old chaplain's gonna react violently and there's gonna be trouble in Yoko City. You mark my words."

"Duly noted," he said.

He had no place to take Susan and no car to get them there, so he returned alone to the BOQ, had a nightcap in the Bachelor's Bar, and hit the rack. The time was still off for him, so it was a restless night of broken sleep punctuated by dreams of Chapel Hill and his father, both dead, not what he needed before he reported to the Black River. Early the next morning he was up, shaving and putting on his dress blues and then heading downstairs for breakfast. After that, he would report in.

The Black River

On December 30, 1967, he put on his heavy overcoat—his 'Venetian' or 'V' coat—and reported for duty aboard the Black River. A grizzled second-class petty officer—a Boatswain's Mate—greeted Jack at the gangplank. The petty officer called below to the Officer of the Day, who came quickly to the quarterdeck, which was an area defined by ropes and a canopy at the top of the gangplank. His name was Paul Sessums, and he was a skinny sallow-faced lieutenant junior grade from New Hampshire by way of Harvard and Navy OCS. He introduced himself and then said, "Welcome aboard."

"Thanks, Paul. Good to be here."

"You're kidding, aren't you? We always say the only officers who show up here are those who made someone mad back at BUPERS or did something wrong at their previous duty station and got shitcanned to this rust bucket. You've got some kind of rough duty ahead of you. I can't wait to get off this tub. It's the roughest ride in the whole damn Navy. Half the crew stays seasick and I'm one of 'em. I can't tell you how bad it is when you get in heavy seas and it's pretty rough even in good seas. And the living conditions are horrible. You'll see."

"Jesus. Can't be that bad, can it?"

"No, it's worse. Come on below and I'll buy you a cup of coffee."

Jack followed him below deck. Inside, the ship was like a submarine: small and tight and warm and muggy. No air. No space. The corridors—passageways—were wide enough for one person. If two men met, one had to brace against a bulkhead for the other to pass. The wardroom was a small compartment with a counter and cabinets at one end and a table bolted to the deck with chairs for eight. The mess table dominated the room. It was covered with a green felt tablecloth that bore the ship's emblem in gold. On the counter were a pot of coffee and a pot of hot water. Both sat on a double-eyed warmer. "The water's for my tea," Sessums said. "I don't drink coffee."

"Hell," Jack said. "The Navy runs on coffee. I'm surprised they let you get away with tea. You could have been court-martialed for a violation of Navy customs and traditions."

Sessums brought in a yeoman, who stamped Jack's orders and noted the time and date he had reported. They sat, and Jack drank the strong black coffee that made him remember the many cups he had on the Princeton, standing watches in the dead of night, watching the sun rise on the four-to-eight morning watch, sink in the late afternoon like an orange ball into the western horizon, so large and hot that you almost thought it would produce steam from the inky-blue water. Jack lit a cigarette. "You want one?" he asked.

Sessums shook his head. "I don't smoke," he said.

"Jesus," Jack said. "You're barely in the Navy. No coffee and no cigarettes. I hope you drink gin. The Pacific fleet runs on gin and black coffee. That's the Navy I know." They sat as Jack drank coffee and smoked, talked about the ship, about the captain—one tough sonofagun, Sessums said, but an outstanding professional and very fair—and the other officers: an engineer, Jason Cohen; a weapons officer, Liam McNamara; a deck officer, Hinky Henderson; the communications officer, T. P. Burwell; Sessums, the operations officer, and a supply officer, Dave Duvall. With the CO and the XO, Robert Yasuto, there were eight in all. All but the captain, Henderson and McNamara, were single and staying in the BOQ, where Jack was. According to Sessums, the ship was rated so unfit for habitation that the officers were allowed to stay ashore in Navy quarters when they put into port. On the Princeton, they had stayed onboard when in port. "Okay," Jack said. "Show me the ship."

"Now?"

"Yeah, now. I want to see what she looks like."

"She looks like shit. We're in holiday routine this whole week. No one's here. I haven't seen the CO since before Christmas. The men are sleeping in when they're here and most of them are in town with whores."

"Let's go, Mr. Sessums," Jack said, clamping down. "I want to see the ship."

"Aye, sir. Then let's do it."

They toured, and Sessums was right. It was a pigsty, and worse, it smelled like one: sweat, dirty clothes, stale air, and filthy bathrooms, or heads, with crap still in the toilets and urinals reeking of piss and puke. The fore-to-aft passageways that ran on each side of ship were lined with racks for the rockets, but the ship rode high in the water because the racks were mostly empty. He had Sessums take him below decks to the engineering spaces, which were greasy and dirty and empty, the two General Motors 1500 horsepower engines sitting still and quiet. And then the bridge, the pilot house, and the chart room forward of the pilot house. This was the navigator's space. It would be where he would have to learn his craft and practice it. Outside on the signals bridge the cold gray day gripped them again. Jack was ready for more coffee and another cigarette.

"Jesus, Paul, does the CO let you get away with this filth?"

"CO's not here. He doesn't know what it's like now. But in all honesty, I have to say that he really doesn't give a shit. He's interested in four things: one is how we fire these rockets. Two is how the ship's engines run. The CO's a former snipe and he loves to deal with the engines and all of that greasy shit below decks. Three is how long it takes the ship to get to general quarters. He's looking for no more than three minutes, and four is how we perform on the bridge. Captain Stockwell is very unforgiving for mistakes on the bridge. A mistake is a guaranteed ass-chewing and he knows how to chew ass. The captain is a master ship-handler but he likes to make us get it underway and bring it in and god knows if you screw it up, he will have your ass. But really, underneath all of the toughness, I think he's a good guy. In the wardroom at meals with us, he keeps it light and does not discuss business. We talk about everything but business: sports, politics, all of it. And out of the wardroom, the only time we ever hear from him is like I say, if someone screws up: the chief engineer or one of us on the bridge or the weapons and gunnery people firing those damn rockets. Then he comes down on you like a sack of nails. He can be one tough bastard. No, scratch that. He *is* one tough Oklahoma cowboy but he's very good at what he does and if you don't screw off or up, you'll do fine with him. Again, I would call him very fair."

"What about his relationship with his XO? What's his name?"

"Robert Yasuto. They do great. They respect each other and get along fine. He backs the XO up one hundred and ten percent. I have to say, that's easy for him to do because the XO is outstanding too. He doesn't have a lot of personality but he's competent as hell."

"Well, I hope I can do as well as Robert and I guarantee you this, I intend to lead by example and praise you when you do well. When you screw up, I'll speak to you in private. I'll never embarrass you."

"Mister Houston"—because he was to be executive officer Sessums addressed him formally, even though at this point in time he was still a lieutenant junior grade, just like Sessums was—"there's a New Year's Eve ball at the officer's club tomorrow night. Most of the wardroom, including the CO, will be there. It's dress blues and a bow tie with miniature medals. You ought to come and meet everyone."

"Okay, will do," he said.

Jack stayed aboard and had lunch with Paul, fresh and hot off the mess decks. There was no separate wardroom galley for the officers. Their food was cooked in the ship's galley and then handed through a half door from the mess decks. Today's fare was bell peppers stuffed with rice and ground beef and covered with tomato sauce. Jack was impressed. "Do you have a steward?"

"Yes. A second class. His name in Delos Reyes. We call him Huck—like the Communist insurgent Huks in the Philippines after World War II—but the men call him Cockroach."

"Behavior or looks?"

"Both. You'll see. He looks like one and he crouches around in dark corners like his namesake, trying to stay out of harm's way, especially out of the CO's."

"Tell me more about the XO."

"He's Japanese. Nice guy. A Nisei. Second or third generation, I think. Spent time in a one of the camps during the war. His family lives in the bay area. I wouldn't say he's particularly tough. He's a detail guy. Very organized. Never smiles. Never laughs. He won't be there New Year's Eve. I think he's visiting with relatives somewhere out on the economy. Supposed to return New Years' Day."

"Anything else?"

"He's a good ship-handler. Good navigator. Supervises gunfire control when we're firing. Good at that, too. All in all, I'd say he's outstanding, like the CO. They are a good leadership team."

"Okay. Good report. Now, if you'll excuse me, I'm still on California time and it's night there, so I think I'll head back to the BOQ and get some rest. Got to get ready for the ball. Maybe I'll meet Cinderella."

Jack slept that afternoon, while outside another cold rain began to fall. It was Thursday night now, and he was worn out, so he had a light dinner at the BOQ and retired early, listening to the rain splatter on the roof of the otherwise deathly quiet building. It was then that he began to believe that he had made a mistake with Melanie, that he loved her more than anything and that he needed her. Especially now. *What in god's name have I done? Oh, Melanie. Christ. What have I done?*

The New Year's Eve dance was on Friday in one of the Officers' Club ballrooms. The CO was there. He wore Navy formal wear: a cutaway navy-blue formal jacket and dark pants striped with gold. "Hello," he said. "I'm Bill Stockwell. I heard you were in town."

"Hello Captain. I think I hear an accent there. Where're you from?"

"I think I hear one, too. I'm from Oklahoma. How about you?"

"Mississippi."

They hit it off immediately. Stockwell was a small guy, tan and skinny and wiry, like a Texas cowboy. He had short blond hair and a 'v' shaped body and a number of brightly-colored medals on his chest. He had gone to the University of Oklahoma, but he remembered watching the '62 Cotton Bowl on TV, which Texas had won 13-7 over Jack's beloved Ole Miss team, breaking Jack's heart and giving the Ole Miss people a long train ride back to Mississippi. Stockwell remembered the large Texas state flag that the Ole Miss band had presented to the Texas student body. "That," Stockwell said, "was one class act."

Suddenly, there was a yank of Jack's arm, and he found himself on the dance floor with the chaplain's wife. "Hello hot body," she said. "Fancy meeting you here."

They began to dance to the thudding sound of the rock and roll music. She put her hands on Jack's hips and pulled him to her. *Oh my god*, he thought. *Here we go again.* And they did go again, but this time there was no chaplain to bail Jack out. He was otherwise engaged, and his wife pulled Jack to her and began banging him. "Hey," he said. "Hadn't we better watch this?"

"I don't give a damn, so why should you? Byron's busy kissing ass and I'm horny. How about it, honey? Can you handle a woman like me?"

"I wouldn't begin to know how," he said. She began to hold him closely, nuzzling his neck with her mouth. "Come on now," he said, pushing her back. "Don't get me in trouble again. What's your name, anyway?"

"Carolyn King, and I'll let you go this time, sweet meat, but I'm telling you, we need to get together. I'll take you out on the economy and show you a time. If you think you can handle me."

Jack pulled away and then moved toward the sideline, shaking his head incredulously. Carolyn King continued to dance. She didn't care that she was alone. Jack swept the room with his eyes. It was dark and smoky. No one seemed to give a damn about her shenanigans, if they even noticed her at all. This was one horny, apparently unhappy-in-her-marriage woman, but she was also one dangerous woman, and Jack didn't need that.

At a table, there was a younger looking woman with her hair rolled into a tall bun. She had strong features, with a prominent nose—he had always been a sucker for prominent noses—and deep brown eyes. The CO and his wife were at her table, along with an older couple. Jack walked over and introduced himself. Stockwell stood up. "This is my wife, Sheila," he said. "And this is the squadron Commodore, Captain Brunini, and his wife, Betty. And this is their daughter, Kitty. This is Jack Houston, soon to be my XO. He's a Mississippian so he's one step ahead of the crowd already. We southerners stick together."

"Oh god," Betty Brunini said. "That Dixie stuff runs deep. Maybe you can get the band to play it."

"I'd love to hear it," Jack said. "I'd probably do a rebel yell."

"Come join us, Jack," Captain Brunini said. "And give us a report from the real world." Brunini was built like a cannon ball and was dark like one, with piercing brown eyes and a head full of gray hair combed back in a pompadour. Confidence and leadership dripped from him like sugarcane molasses. The Commodore's wife, Betty, was slightly taller than her husband, with brown hair and hazel eyes and an angular face set in a perpetual smile. She was the quintessential Navy wife, made so by the many moves endured by Navy wives, with household goods and children to place in a new school and a new house every two or three years. She looked at Jack with warmth, and he liked her immediately.

The next day, he wrote to Melanie, told her the ship was like, what it would be doing, what he would be doing. He didn't invite her out. He needed to take a tour on the Vietnam gunline to see whether he could handle bringing her out. He hoped—prayed—that he could, but he just didn't know.

Melanie

Upon her return from San Francisco, Melanie told her roommate: "It was a disaster. I went out there hoping to marry him only to find out that he's not marrying me, or anyone else for that matter. It's not that he's married to the Navy. He's married to himself. He can't see beyond the end of his nose in terms of his relationship with me or any other woman. It just breaks my heart."

Susan Crawford, her roommate, looked at Melanie, who was in tears, choking down cries. "It all goes back to that damn history professor throwing him out of class. If it weren't for that, he'd still be in school," Susan said.

"No, I don't think so. He was out of money and he hated being a student here. He might have gone back to Ole Miss to law school—borrowed the money—but I don't think he'd have stuck around here. He—after three years in the Navy—just wasn't cut out for the graduate student's life. Maybe the law student's. I don't know. Maybe nothing but the Navy."

"What's he doing in the Navy? Where is he?"

"He wrote that his ship was in Japan. He said they were leaving for Vietnam soon. I haven't written him back. I'm too damn mad to. I'm just sick of being tossed around and used like an old dishrag."

Susan stared out into the muzzy North Carolina winter's day. "Well, what are you going to do, Melanie?" She paused, still staring into the gloom. "I know what I'd do. I'd find someone else."

Melanie had quit crying. She was in a slip, and she stood up and pulled on a plaid, Villager skirt and a blouse that she buttoned all the way up to her throat and some penny loafers and knee socks. "Damn," she said. "Jack wrote. He's gonna be over there for two years. It's the heart of darkness. Going up those rivers. Shooting rockets. I don't know what all but I do know this. I'm not a part of his plans so I'm moving on. There's a Jewish guy named Mark Goldberg who wants to date me. He's been asking me out since we got here. I guess I'll try it. Anything's better than sitting in this dorm room. Even Mark Goldberg."

Chapter Four
The First Cruise

Bill Stockwell was a lieutenant commander, one grade higher than Jack would be when his promotion to lieutenant finally caught up with him. Stockwell sat in the captain's chair on the bridge, a quiet, competent professional. It was January 3, 1968, and they were in sea and anchor detail status, which is the operation they performed for getting underway or coming into port. Liam McNamara had the conn, which meant that he would drive the ship. Paul Sessums was in the Combat Information Center, which they called 'CIC', working the maneuvering board, from which he could calculate courses and speeds necessary to avoid collisions. The main deck officer was Hinky Henderson. He was responsible for the boatswain mates, who would take in lines and help get the ship underway. Yasuto, the XO/navigator, was stationed at a chart on which he would plot the ship's movement and recommend courses to get the Black out of Yokosuka Harbor and into Tokyo Bay for the not-uneventful ride down that beehive of nautical activity. T. P. Burwell was in the 'radio shack', and Dave Duvall was there with Burwell. Jack stood with Yasuto.

It was a smooth operation. McNamara expertly ordered in all lines except number three and used his engines and rudders to 'breast' out from the pier. Since the Black was tied up port side to the pier, McNamara put his starboard engine ahead one-third and his port engine back one-third with his rudders to port. The Black's stern pushed away from the pier, and McNamara took in line three. He went all back one-third with his rudders amidships, which moved the Black away from the pier. He then went ahead one-third on both engines and began using his rudders to steer her. The XO, Yasuto, began feeding him course recommendations, and the bridge team's performance was an exercise in excellence and professionalism.

Jack recalled his experiences on the Princeton getting underway and coming into tie up. Captain T. J. 'Black Tom' Gallagher, a World War II aviator, would raise hell both times about sailboats and civilian cargo ships that dared to cross his path. The bridge would thus be a cesspool of curses and excitement and above all else, fear, because if Gallagher as much as thought someone was not performing up to his standards, it was a string of curses that would make a Marine Drill Sergeant at Parris Island—generally the most creative cursers in the armed forces—grin in unabashed admiration.

They started down Tokyo Bay. There were ships and boats everywhere. None of them seemed to know the Rules of the Nautical Road, which governed every situation involving ships underway: meeting, crossing and overtaking. Stockwell sat quietly then said, "Begin sounding the ship's horn: one long blast every three minutes and maintain your speed at two-thirds. Follow the XO's recommendations. Mr. Sessums in CIC will work the maneuvering board and advise you on avoiding these freighters. You know the drill, Mr. McNamara. Okay, secure from sea and anchor detail. Set the regular watch. The bridge watch will remain the same. Go to it gentlemen."

They moved silently down the bay. Stockwell sat and watched, and his team performed superbly. Yasuto navigated on a chart of the bay and made course recommendations to get them out of there. Sessums fed McNamara information about approaching ships, telling him which ship had the right-of-way and what the Black's role would be in the encounter: maneuver—the privileged ship—or maintain course and speed—the burdened ship. It was like a symphony, every musical instrument working together to produce a harmonious sound, and it was a beautiful operation to watch. Stockwell obviously had enough confidence in his team and his training of them to let them run the show, and they did.

On the Black, life settled into a predictable routine: breakfast in the wardroom, work 0800 to 1200. Dinner on the mess decks and in the wardroom, work until 1630. Supper in the wardroom and on the mess decks. The meals were good: eggs, ham, bacon, sausage, hash browns, toast or biscuits for breakfast. Dinner was beef tips on noodles, meatloaf, hamburgers and hot dogs, roast beef, potatoes, string beans, baked beans, biscuits, baked ham, round steak. Supper was make-your-own-sandwich with an assortment of meats, French fries, a hearty vegetable soup, chili. Delos Reyes served them. When they came into the wardroom for a meal, Delos Reyes had set the table.

Navy every day china, navy cutlery, a large white tablecloth with an officer's crest in the center. A cook in the ship's galley handed the plates through a window to Delos Reyes, who took the plates and set them before the officers, starting with the captain. Subsequently, Delos Reyes placed refill bowls on the table, from which the officers could replenish. The meal was followed by dessert—cobbler with ice cream, various pies, cakes and always, more ice cream. Then came coffee, and those who smoked lit up. At 2000, there was a movie in the wardroom, and they sat and drank more coffee and smoked and watched their lone—besides mail—connection to 'the world'.

Jack stayed in the JO bunk room, which had eight bunks crammed into a stateroom about 250 square feet. The space was air-conditioned and heated, depending on the season, but it still managed to be smelly and damp. The JO's slept in there when they were not on watch or working the 0800-1630 workday or dining in the wardroom. They played gin rummy on the one table in the middle and did sit ups and pushups on the deck. Jack settled in with them and told them stories about Ole Miss and Mississippi, about race and the White Citizens Council and his father, who had been the Mayor of Concord. He told them how his father had interacted with the Citizens Council and with Sophie Cleary Brown, the firebrand editor of the local newspaper who had won a Pulitzer Prize in 1964. He, too, did exercises on the deck, and he felt his stomach tightening and his arms strengthening. He ate three squares in the wardroom, and walked the ship and pushed the officers to get their spaces and heads cleaned up. The ship gradually began to round into shape. Yasuto and Stockwell were oblivious.

They sailed south by Okinawa, passed Iwo Jima and headed down the east side of Taiwan. Then they turned right and, skirting the northern coast of Luzon, went west across the inky-blue waters of the South China Sea. Soon they were out of the range of the radar, and it was time for celestial navigation. Yasuto taught Jack all of it: how to use the sextant—the mariner's friend since ancient times—how to use the chronometer, Loran and the depth finder, all combining to give them a 'fix', a position in the vast expanse of ocean. Jack was a fast learner, and the last two days of the cruise he did it all. They headed for Cam Ranh Bay.

The officers, other than Dave Duvall—supply officers did not stand bridge watches—stood watches one-in-four: on one watch and off three watches. All of the watches were four hours except the two 'dog' watches from 1600 to

1800 and 1800 to 2000, split that way so those two officers could have supper. The XO—and thus Jack—did not stand watches but got up before sunrise and 'shot' stars and again at evening twilight.

In his rack, Jack thought of Melanie: of her smell, of her feel, of her gentle touch. He thought of her unconditional love, which he had never experienced from a loved one. Never. He thought about San Francisco, and he now knew that he had blown it, blown a chance to have her for life and waiting for him in Yokosuka, and it made him sad. *Jesus. Why didn't I tell her I would bring her out once I got settled? What in the fuck was I thinking? I didn't do it and I may have lost her. Forever. But maybe not. Maybe I can get back to her and tell her to come out and it'll be all right. I'll do it at some point. But first I've got to get through at least the first part of this cruise and learn what my job is. Then I'll do it. I promise, Melanie. I swear to myself that I will do that. It's not too late.*

They awakened him thirty minutes before dawn, and he dressed—working khakis and a piss cutter cap—and went to the bridge for morning twilight and the last stars of the night. On the bridge, he would have his first cup of coffee and his first cigarette of the new day, and he would find the first magnitude stars and mark them mentally then glue his eyes on what would become the horizon when first light came. Yasuto had taught him and taught him well.

At first light, he would begin shooting stars. His quartermaster assistant would identify each star that was low on the horizon, and he found it on the scope of the sextant, 'swung' the bottom of the sextant from side to side, then, using a device on the side of the sextant, brought the star 'down to the horizon'. He called out the reading on the sextant, and the quartermaster called out the time on the ship's chronometer. The messenger of the watch wrote down the name of the star, the time and Jack's sextant reading. After six or so stars, Jack would watch the sun—a lurid orange ball—rising on the eastern horizon, behind them, then he would retire to the pilot house where he would feed his readings into the charts in a large book, then apply the calculations from the book to locate a spot on the chart. When he had four reasonably close spots, he would draw lines to connect them, and where they crossed, he would have his 'fix', from which he could adjust the ship's course to reach Cam Ranh Bay.

He loved it, and in the early morning light, with his sextant and coffee, he felt a connection to all of the old mariners who had gone before him and a sense of awe at the power of the sextant and its age and the fact that it was still the essence of navigating a ship in the expanse of the sea. After his plot, he would send the latitude and longitude to the CO and then retire to the wardroom for breakfast. There would be juice and more coffee—hot and black—and the officers would hang around there until 0800, kibitzing and smoking and telling lies about conquests ashore. Then it was time to meet with their divisions and give orders for the day. And so once again, the cycle would begin: work, watches—the enlisted men also stood one-in-four watches—dinner, knock off ship's work at 1630, free time, supper, movie, rack time. Those who had the midwatch—midnight to 0400—hit their racks at 1630 and slept until it was time to get up for their watch. Having skipped supper, they ate 'midrats', midnight rations, before their watches, the worst of the day. After that grueling watch, it was back to sleep for a couple of hours before reveille.

The wardroom was a happy place, and Jack looked forward to the meals. He engaged the captain in talks about college football: old games, players from the past, teams they both knew, plays they remembered, coaches, stadiums. Bill Stockwell enjoyed these discussions, and they talked about what was going on back in the States: music—Jack knew the latest—clothes and politics. They talked about ports: Subic Bay, Hong Kong and Yokosuka, which, although they were home-ported there in theory, they saw only occasionally because of the requirements of the gunline.

The crew, except for the chief petty officers, slept in a large berthing space all the way forward. Sleeping in the bow, when the ship went into strong seas from ahead, they moved up and down like yoyos. Their head was forward, too, but it was too small for that many men—the Black carried about 140 enlisted men—and it stayed filthy except when they cleaned it each morning. No one—before Jack—had ever inspected it, however, so the morning cleaning had been cursory at best.

The Black's men wore denim, dark blue bell-bottom pants and light blue denim long-sleeved shirts. Their shoes were Boondockers, like the shoes that Jack had worn at OCS and at Chapel Hill. The Boondockers were ankle-high, and the men wore dark socks. In cold weather, they wore 'P' coats. During the workday, the enlisted men performed work in connection with their specialty: navigation, gunnery, deck, engineering, supply and communications: cleaning and operating the equipment, chipping and painting, running the ship's store, processing payroll, preparing meals, navigating the ship, raising and lowering signal flags and operating the signal lights when they encountered another vessel.

Bill Stockwell split his time between the bridge and his stateroom, which was also his office. While on the bridge, he was a keen observer of the officer-of-the-deck—the OOD—and any misstep would draw his ire and a lesson in whatever function the OOD had bungled. They fired the rockets, the five-inch gun, the fifty-caliber machine guns, and the two forty-millimeter pom-pom guns every day. They called the pom-pom guns 'forty mike-mikes'. The ship went to general quarters for the firing exercises, and Stockwell put a clock on the time it took them to assume battle stations and secure the ship for combat. They were good. Damn good. And there was never a problem with their time.

The Black moved southwest, its radar searching for land and easier navigation, and Robert Yasuto and Jack hoped that their celestial navigation would bring them to the right spot.

Chapter Five
Cam Ranh Bay

Cam Ranh Bay is a large west-to-east indention off the South China Sea that cuts sharply into the underbelly of South Vietnam. It lies about halfway between the DMZ on the north and the tip of the Mekong Delta on the south. Cam Ranh is one of the finest natural harbors in the world, and the U.S. military had taken it over early in the war, just as had the Japanese in World War II and the French before and after them. The Russian Imperial Fleet on the way to its Waterloo at Tsushima Straits had stopped there in 1906. Entering from the east, the bay, about a mile in, opens into a large north-south expanse. The Navy took the portion of the harbor at the southeast end of the bay, nearest the South China Sea, which included the prime beachfront along the ocean and slightly inland, a small harbor with a single pier and barges for ammo loadouts. To the north of the Navy base, the Air Force and the Army had large bases that dwarfed the Navy's small presence on the prime real estate at the south end of the harbor. The Navy was good at getting the best.

    Jack navigated the Black east into the bay and then brought her south on a course that would take them toward the Navy pier. A half-mile or so out from the pier, the captain asked Jack if he wanted to take her in to the pier. Knowing he had no choice, he answered affirmatively and took the conn. Fear churned in his gut. He had always hated ship handling—he was terrified of running the ship aground, or into a pier, or some other egregious ship handling act—and now here he was, about to try to drive the Black River into a narrow slot alongside a small pier in Cam damn Ranh friggin' Bay South Damn Vietnam. And only six weeks before, he had been ejected from a history class at the University of North Carolina. Jesus. How had it come to this so quickly?

    He ran the ship on a course parallel to the shoreline and then turned her left to port ninety degrees on a course that would take her alongside the pier. No problem. Jack began his run at the pier, to which he would attempt to tie the

Black up on the ship's port, or left, side. No problem. He had the wind behind him. He had the ship all ahead one-third, or moving about 150 yards a minute. No problem. Plenty of time in which to stop the ship. He had the pier bore sighted off his port bow. Beyond it lay the beach. He had to bring her alongside the pier and stop her in time to avoid running her up onto the beach. No problem.

"All back one-third," he said. The ship kept moving ahead. "All back two-thirds," he shouted. The ship kept moving forward, toward the pier. *Oh god no, the trailing wind is pushing us forward.* Jack froze, afraid to go back on the engines anymore, convinced that the two-thirds would be sufficient to bail him out. With savage suddenness, the pier loomed ahead. Jack had waited too long. He was headed for the pier, the bow aimed at its center point. The Black rolled on, high and hard. Behind him, he could hear the captain talking. "Slow it down. Slow it down," Stockwell said softly.

Then the CO shouted: "This is the captain. I have the conn. All engines back full, emergency." On the pier, the line handlers scattered like a covey of quail, running for their lives. The engines took hold, but it was too late. The USS Black River slammed into the pier with a horrible splintering sound. On the main deck, deckhands ran fore and aft, trying to get large blocking dummies over the side to cushion the impact. It wasn't enough. Nothing was enough. Splinters from the wooden pier pilings flew like shrapnel—everywhere. The Black's deckhands dived for cover, dodging incoming wood shrapnel. The captain finally got the ship stopped, but there were no longer any line handlers to receive the lines and tie her up.

Yasuto took the bullhorn and bellowed: "On the pier there. You men get back out here and handle those lines." The Black settled in next to the pier snugly, and the captain sounded the ship's horn. The line handlers came chugging down the pier again, took the lines, looped them over metal cleats, and made the Black fast, looking up at the bridge the whole time to see what mad fool had almost killed them. The Black and the pier had both survived, but Jack's ego had not. He had failed his first shiphandling test, and every junior officer and enlisted man on the ship would know that their new XO couldn't drive their ship worth a damn.

Jack formally relieved Yasuto, who caught the first plane out of Cam Ranh for the huge American air base at Tan Son Nhut near Saigon, and with his JO's, Jack headed for the Cam Ranh Bay Navy Officers' Club. It was on a sandy beach facing the South China Sea, an elevated wooden structure with a long porch surrounded by palm trees and sand. They sat on the porch and drank gin gimlets and smoked and talked about round-eyed women and about the whores they had screwed in the Philippines, Hong Kong, Taiwan and Japan. "Damn Sessums is such an Ichabod Crane that he can't even get a whore to screw him. And Henderson, hell, he's got such a little pecker that they come back in the bar laughing afterward." The speaker was Jason Cohen, an acerbic Jewish guy whom Jack had already pegged as a troublemaker. He was the engineer and forever looked greasy from his vocation. Cohen was a miniature Bluto, heavyset, swarthy, with a perpetual five o'clock shadow. His beard was so thick that it was impossible to shave it off. Married, he still frequented the whores of the Far East.

Liam McNamara was a large heavyset Boston Irishman, who had played football at the Naval Academy with Roger Staubach. Liam had a square face, a pug nose, sandy hair and blue eyes. He snorted. "Hell, Goldberg, none of 'em want to screw a Jew. You couldn't even kiss a girl with that schnoz you got. It's bigger than your dick. You oughta break it just to flatten it out a little bit."

They drank on. Evening twilight came, and the South China Sea turned from indigo blue to a depressing inky color, while the waves picked up with the evening tide and crashed into the beach. "You see that little house down there, XO?" Dave Duvall, the supply officer asked. He was a tall drink of water with a shock of brown hair and no lips, with recessed eyes guarded by heavy dark eyebrows. He looked like a corpse. Some of them in fact said he was dead in the water, so they called him 'Dead'.

"Yeah, I see it, Dave. What about it?"

"That's Admiral Zumwalt's weekend place. Comes down here from Saigon with his Navy nurse girlfriend and shacks up. When we're in on a weekend, you'll see them swimming down there. She's got a body that won't wait."

"Damn," Jack said. "You sure it's Zumwalt?"

"Hell yes. His aide stays in the officer's quarters here. He comes over here drinking sometime. Good guy. He's a southerner, too. I think from South Carolina. Sounds a little like you, XO, but not as southern." Jack studied the hooch and wondered what Zumwalt's staff officers thought of the arrangement. The Black's officers drank some more, and all of the Zumwalt stuff disappeared into an alcohol-fueled haze.

They stumbled back to the ship through the thick, damp night air, over the hill that separated the ocean beach from the bay itself, then down the slick-with-grease pier to the ship. Drunk, Jack ordered the deck apes to 'cast off' the lines holding the ship in place instead of ordering them to 'take in' the lines, but eventually he got the ship underway and took her out to an anchorage in the bay where they would load rockets off barges the next day. And around noon, three feet lower in the water, they got underway and headed south for the tip of the Mekong Delta peninsula, cut between it and Con Son Island, home of the infamous monkey-cage prisons, then northwest into the green waters of the Gulf of Siam and Phu Quoc Island, the Black's first firing mission of this tour on the gunline.

Phu Quoc

The green island rose jarringly out of the sea, and as they moved closer, Jack could see imposingly high cliffs that soared above narrow sandy beaches. At the east end of the island, there was a small harbor with an opening just wide enough to admit a small vessel like the Black River. Anything larger had to anchor outside and use small craft—lighterage—to load or offload material in support of the military operations ashore. The Black River shot through the slot and anchored near the rusting hulk of an old LST that had been converted into a large dormitory for the American troops who worked with the ARVN—Army of the Republic of Vietnam—forces in search and destroy missions against the Viet Cong, who, Jack had been told, operated with near impunity throughout the island. Scattered around the small harbor were several Navy swift boats. Their crews lounged about the boats in shorts, soaking up the hot tropical sun, drinking beer, smoking and swearing gratuitously.

Stockwell eyed the swift boat crews suspiciously. "I ought to go over there and rip them a new one," he said to McNamara. "But I've got better things to do. Get my boat ready. I'm going in to talk to the local ARVN chieftain and see what they want us to do."

He left in the Black's motor whaleboat. For the crew, Jack ordered swim call with a shark watch, and several men with M-1 rifles took up positions around the ship with instructions to fire at any fin they saw. Then Jack retired to his stateroom to drink a Coke and smoke a cigarette and plow through the endless paperwork that constituted the administrative part of his job: reports, requests for leave or transfer, disciplinary matters, the never-ending administrative detritus that kept the ship running and that the Navy loved. He called the bridge and ordered them to secure swim call and get the men back on board. Then, he listened to Armed Forces Radio out of Saigon and the music he had left behind in the States—the Beatles and 'Hey Jude', Otis Redding and 'Sittin' on the Dock of the Bay', and his favorite, 'Angel of the Morning'—and he wallowed in his sadness and loneliness and against the knife's edge of self-pity. He had left too much behind. And he had given up too much. And now he was here, in the middle of darkness and crippling depression. But he had to go on. Quitting was not an option.

The explosion came out of nowhere, and the Black shuddered from the force of it as the percussion radiated through the waters of the harbor. Another followed, and by the time he reached the bridge, the swift boats were underway, and the Black River's men were already manning their combat stations. Liam McNamara had ordered the ship to general quarters and the anchor retrieved. The XO stood and watched as the men moved flawlessly to get the ship in fighting condition and underway. The Black might look like a scow, Jack thought, but her crew knew how to get her ready to fight—in a hurry. There was no sign of the captain or the motor whaleboat.

"What about the captain, Liam?"

"We can't wait, XO. We gotta get the hell out of the harbor before they find us with those mortar rounds. Whatcha wanta do?"

"Take her out, Liam. I'll take responsibility if there's a problem."

McNamara rang up engineering on the sound-powered phone. "How close are you to being up and running, Jason?" He was silent. "Okay, standby. We're getting the hell out of here. As soon as they get the anchor up, be prepared to give us everything you got."

Jack watched the sea and anchor detail working from the bow to bring the anchor up. "The anchor's breaking ground, sir," came the report from the quartermaster on the sound-powered phone with the Boatswains Mates on the forecastle. "Very well. Let's get the hell out of here," McNamara replied. "All engines ahead full. Right standard-rudder."

McNamara headed the ship for the slot, and Jack took over navigation from the quartermaster, giving McNamara a course through the narrow opening. The Black's two diesel engines roared to life, and the ship shuddered and moved forward. "I'll go to flank as soon as we clear the slot," McNamara said.

"Sir, the captain's behind us in the motor whaleboat. He's chasing us," one of the quartermasters shouted from the wing.

Jack moved to the rear of the bridge. The captain *was* in the motor whaleboat, waving his arms. "Whatta you think, Liam? Should we stop to get him?"

Behind them more explosions rocked the small harbor. The swift boats had roared out ahead of the Black River. A tug attached by lines to the old LST hull had begun towing it out to sea. The captain stood astride the motor whaleboat, waving his arms for the Black to go on.

"Let's get through the slot, XO. Then we can take him aboard. They hit us in here and with three thousand rockets below decks, and church will be out for this ship. That okay?"

"Okay with me," he said. "Let her rip."

McNamara took her through the slot and then slowed to take the skipper aboard. With the mortars crashing, Stockwell came aboard. He came onto the bridge. "Great job XO, Liam. You did the right thing. They can replace me a helluva lot easier than they can replace the ship."

Stockwell lit a cigarette. "Take her around the east side of the island, Liam. We're gonna do some shooting up the coast."

Liam McNamara ordered a 180 and headed east then turned north and headed up the east side of Phu Quoc Island. "How far, sir?"

"We'll go up about six miles. There's an outcropping up there. Does it show on the chart, XO?"

"Yessir, Captain."

"Are we going to try to take out those mortars, Captain?" Jack asked.

"No, XO, we got bigger fish to fry."

About a half-hour up the east coast, Jack picked up the outcropping. He navigated the Black alongside it, then Stockwell said, "All engines stop, Liam."

Jack went below to his station in the Combat Information Center. There, the radio crackled with the voice of an airborne spotter. The spotter gave them coordinates on a map, and the gunner, Gunner's Mate First Class Wallis, fed them into a fire control system and then set the port side launchers. "Ready, XO," Wallis said.

"Very well." To the bridge, Jack reported, "Combat is ready."

He heard Paul Sessums report ready to the captain then a muffled response, and Sessums said "You are cleared to fire, XO."

"Very well, Mr. Sessums. Launchers 1, 3, 5 and 7: one salvo, high explosive, fuse quick. Fire!"

Wallis repeated the command to the launchers, and all hell broke loose. There was an enormous swoosh, and four five-inch rockets screamed toward the island, where they were to clear the escarpment and hammer the hell out of the Viet Cong.

They didn't. The rockets slammed into the cliffs and exploded, "What happened, Liam?" the captain asked. "Did we have the range wrong?"

"I don't know, Sir. Lemme go below and check with Wallis."

McNamara scrambled down the ladder to CIC, where the speaker box came to life. "Can you tell what the problem is, XO?" Stockwell spoke softly.

It was strange. Jack felt like it was his high school football coach talking, and he felt the old fear—the fear of making a mistake, of being wrong—churning deep inside of him. He spoke, "Captain, Mr. McNamara is telling us what happened up there. We're going to check Wallis's input into the fire control system. That's all I can tell you at this point."

"Very well, XO. Just let me know."

"What happened, Liam?"

"I've checked Wallis's input. The range is correct but the arc of the rockets at that range is not high enough to clear these cliffs so the rockets went into the cliffs."

"What if we took the ship farther out? Would that give the rockets time enough to reach their apex and clear the cliffs?"

"That's a great idea, XO. It's certainly worth a try."

"How high are the cliffs, Mr. McNamara?"

"About 400 yards, I'd guess."

"And how far below the top did we hit?"

McNamara thought. "I'd guess a couple of hundred yards."

"And what's the range to the cliffs, Bowden?"

Bowden checked the radar.

"Exactly a half-mile, XO. A thousand yards."

"And what's the apex of the rockets at this range, Wallis?"

"Twenty-five hundred and forty feet, XO."

Jack did some calculations and switched on the squawk box. "Captain, we're too close in. The rockets don't have time to reach an altitude sufficient to clear the cliffs. We need to move out some so the rockets can get high enough to clear the cliffs. Can you have Mr. Sessums move her out about a thousand yards? We'll do a new plot and I believe we can clear the cliffs then."

"Very well, XO. We'll give it a shot. XO, give us a course and talk us in to the new spot."

"Aye, Sir." Jack began feeding information to the bridge on the sound-powered phone, and within minutes the Black was in new position.

Bowden was the plotter. "Okay, Bowden, give us a new range and direction to the target."

Bowden fed the range and direction information to Wallis, who cranked it into the fire controller.

"We're ready, Captain," Jack reported over the speaker.

"Okay, XO. Let her rip."

"Aye, Sir. Let's fire one launcher and see if we clear before we waste four rockets."

"Very well."

This time the rocket arched high over the cliffs. "Okay, XO, you cleared it. Tell Mr. McNamara to come on back up here and tell the airborne spotter we're ready to adjust fire."

The spotter then began directing the lone launcher, right one hundred, add one hundred until finally, "Give me four launchers, two salvos each, fire for effect."

Eight rockets screamed out of the launchers and over the cliffs.

The radio crackled. "Way to friggin' go," the spotter said. "Right on top of those bastards. Blew some of 'em apart. Give me eight more. Four launchers, two salvos each."

On the bridge, the captain asked, "Did you figure that out, Mr. McNamara?"

"No sir. The XO did. On a piece of paper. Basic geometry, he said."

The squawk box crackled. "Way to go, XO. That was brilliant. Way to improvise."

"Thanks, Captain. I think we got 'em now."

But the 'blew apart' comment took him to a dark place, the USS Princeton, which carried a battalion landing team of about 1,500 Marines. Jack was on the bridge, second on the watch, when the speaker crackled that there had been an incident on the mess decks. The captain was on the bridge, and in accordance with the ship's—and the Navy's—custom and procedure, dispatched Jack—the junior officer of the watch—to go check it out.

Half of the Marine was on the mess decks. The other half had gone up to the hangar deck. It was a bomb elevator, and the Marine had put the garbage on it, pushed the start button about three feet from the elevator and tried to dive onto the elevator. He was a flash too slow, and it cut him in half. Guts were sliding around the mess decks, propelled by the ship's motion. Blood spread ghoulishly across the decks. The Marine's lower half was still pretty much intact. The cook gang stood and looked. Jack ordered them back to the galley and called the bridge. The ship's public address system roared: "Supply officer to the mess decks. Gunnery officer to the mess decks. Executive officer to the mess decks."

There was an investigation. The senior, career officers tried to pin the blame on Jack's roommate, Charlie Holt. He was a reserve and, so they thought, had nothing to lose. In the end, the Navy's bureaucracy buried the investigation, and the paperwork was fed into a great furnace somewhere in the bowels of the ship. Charlie Holt escaped unscathed. Actually, Holt had thought about staying in. The dead Marine on the mess decks put an end to that. Jack shook his head at the memories and returned to the present.

The Black moved up the east coast of Phu Quoc, firing into the evening. As they finished the firing mission, a small motor whaleboat made its way toward them across the now-inky water of the Gulf of Thailand. It was the island commander, and he brought a mother lode of live lobsters. Rain began to pelt them as they pulled away from the island. The ship's cooks boiled the lobsters in the Black's galley, and Stockwell authorized use of the ship's cache of medicinal whiskey to precede dinner in the officer's mess. Afterward, they sat and drank Navy coffee and smoked the captain's Schimmel Pennic cigars and listened to music on Armed Forces Radio out of Saigon: The Four Tops, the Temptations, Mason's Williams's 'Classical Gas', all of it flooding the XO with memories of his time out of the service, of his time with Melanie, of doing the Carolina shag and the boogaloo and listening to beach music: 'Sixty Minute Man' and 'Carolina Girls'. He now knew that he had made a mistake. *I should have asked Melanie to marry me,* he thought. *Brought her out here. Gotten us a place to live. Jesus. How could I be so stupid? How could I screw it up so badly? I love her. I need her but I'm not going to have her. At least not now.*

Jack ached. And he longed for what he had left behind. He thought about resigning his commission and going home, but he knew that wouldn't work. *I'll invite her out to get married. That's what I'll do. And she'll come and it'll all work out and it'll be okay. I'll write her now. It's gonna be all right. I just know it will.*

Rock Jaw

Its name was Rach Gia, but the Americans called it Rock Jaw, because its letters suggested that pronunciation, and it looked on the chart like the silhouette of a man's face with a big jaw jutting out. It sat on the west coast of the Vietnam Mekong peninsula, north of the Mekong Delta, and it was rocky and just below the Vietnam border with Cambodia. Rock Jaw sat at the confluence of several branches of the Ho Chi Minh trail, and U. S. forces were constantly trying to interdict and stop the flow of men and material into South Vietnam, mostly unsuccessfully. The North Vietnamese who used the trail switched from one branch to another, and they moved at night.

An amphibious squadron of ships: an LPH like the Princeton; an APA: an armored personnel carrier, an LSD—a landing ship dock—and an LST, a landing ship tank, had put a battalion of Marines ashore to take on the North Vietnamese coming down the trail. The 1500 Marines were at Rock Jaw, but it was overcast and rainy, and they could not get close air support in to hammer a North Vietnamese regiment that had pushed them back against the sea and was using artillery to hammer them. The Black's mission was to give them the fire support that they so desperately needed.

Jack navigated them in to 500 yards off the beach, so they could use their twelve-inch, short-range rockets, and the Marines on the line began calling for fire. The Black fired four launchers constantly, moving its fire up and down the Marine line in accordance with directions from the shore. Still, the North Vietnamese, outstanding soldiers that they were, fought doggedly on, always pushing, always probing the Marine line for weakness, and always attacking. The Marines held. North Vietnamese artillery rounds began splashing around the Black. Stockwell maneuvered her to avoid, but the splashes came closer and closer. Stockwell began zigzagging the Black like the destroyer he had driven. In and out, up and down the line, bobbing and weaving like Muhammad Ali. The North Vietnamese artillery couldn't hit her. The Black kept firing. Her big rockets screamed in over the Marines into the North Vietnamese ranks. The explosions gave them pause, but the line of battle was about two miles long, and the Black couldn't fire everywhere at once.

Two destroyers showed up to supplement the Black's fire from about three miles out. The water was too shallow for them to move in any closer, and firing their five-inch guns—with a range of over 10,000 yards—they didn't need to. The destroyers were good—very good—but they could not deliver the firepower with the rapidity or explosive power of the Black's fire. Finally, at 35 knots came on the USS New Jersey, the big mama of the Seventh Fleet. She had come west to Vietnam for a situation just like this, and it was now her time. The old lady opened up with her sixteen-inch guns from about five nautical miles out, and for the North Vietnamese, church was out. The New Jersey's sixteen-inch shells came like screaming freight cars over the lesser ships like the Black River and exploded upon contact, taking out a ridge here, a hill there. The combined naval gunfire of four United States Navy ships was too much for anyone, and it was far too much for the North Vietnamese regiment that had foolishly attacked a Marine battalion within the range of naval gunfire. It chewed them up and spit them out, and the survivors fled inland from the holocaust that had enveloped them on the rocky rises and hidden swales of Rock Jaw.

When the firing ended, the Black received a radio message from the New Jersey: would you come out and put on a firing demonstration for us. We want to call the crew topside to see it. Dusk had come, and the indigo sky would provide a perfect backdrop for the Black's streaking rockets. Stockwell said yes, and the Black moved out close to the New Jersey. The two destroyers pulled up. The Black's crew manned all eight launchers, and Jack called for them to fire four salvos into the day's waning light.

It was New Year's Eve all over the country rolled into one fusillade. Fired forward at a 45-degree-angle off the bow, 32 twelve-inch rockets streaked out into the ambient air and with white phosphorous—Willy Pete the sailors called it—and proximity fuses that caused the rockets to explode above the water, the Black put on a light show of leviathan proportions. When it was over, the New Jersey's crew shouted and applauded, and she sounded her horn over and over.

The admiral on board The Big J nominated the Black River for Seventh Fleet 'ship of the year', and she won. Because of the risk that the Black had taken going in close, and with the hostile fire she had taken, Bill Stockwell received a bronze star with combat 'V' for valor. Jack received a Navy Commendation Medal with combat V, and the other officers Navy Achievement Medals, also with combat V's. The Black herself received a Navy Unit Commendation.

The Pueblo

On January 23, 1968, the North Koreans attacked and captured the USS Pueblo, a spy ship that was conducting surveillance off its coast. The commanding officer, under heavy fire from North Korean gunboats, surrendered, and the North Koreans took the ship into port and imprisoned the crew to what would later be revealed as horrible treatment. In the wardroom, the Black's officers talked about the Pueblo's capture.

"Why didn't we send out air cover, I wonder?" T. P. Burwell asked.

"I understand that they went on standby at Tachikawa but then decided not to send them," Bill Stockwell said. "I don't know why other than I think Washington all the way up to the White House was involved and likely didn't want a confrontation with North Korea."

Jack: "But why didn't Captain Bucher try to get away? Why did he surrender?"

"I don't know, XO, but he wasn't armed and I think he wanted to avoid the loss of life."

"But at what cost? Jesus, all of that top-secret gear and information thrown right in the North Koreans' hands. Man, that's an intelligence disaster of the first magnitude."

"What would you have done, Captain?" Liam McNamara asked.

"Well, it's easy for me to sit here and say I would have done this and that but until you're in that situation it's impossible to say. What about you, XO?"

"Captain, I would have headed her out to sea and made them sink me and then try to save as many as I could. I'll be damned if I would have surrendered her."

Stockwell laughed. "Well, men, we've got a fighting XO. XO, I hope you never have to make that decision."

"I do, too, and of course, with the Black River, we've got plenty of firepower. But if it ever happened to us, I would fight those sonofabitches with everything we've got until they sank us."

"Way to go, XO," Dave Duvall added. "Way to go. But what would you fight with?"

"Well, to start off, the five-inch gun, the forty mike-mikes and the fifty caliber machine guns. And If I lost them, I'd use the rockets."

"How would you do that?"

"Well, it'd be like the old sailing ship days. I'd level them off and broadside them like the sailing ships used to do. Just pull up alongside them and blast away with proximity fuses."

"Well, good luck with that, XO," Liam McNamara said. "I think they'd blow you out of the water before you could do that."

"Well, maybe. But I'd go down trying."

Chapter Six
Subic Bay

They finished their firing in IV Corps and then, in late January 1968, headed east across the South China Sea to Subic Bay, on the west side of Luzon. It was here that the Spanish fleet had holed up before returning to Manila Bay and a crushing defeat at Cavite, where Dewey had famously told Captain Gridley of the USS Olympia, "You may fire when ready, Gridley." And Gridley had, and he fired hard. Dewey's squadron sank almost the entire Spanish fleet, although it was a mismatch from the start, as Dewey had newer ships, and the Spanish fleet never left the piers where they were tied up. Jack had been there when he was on the Princeton, had been to Corregidor and seen Malinta Tunnel, where MacArthur—'Dugout Doug', they called him—holed up during the Japanese assault against the American troops fighting on the Bataan Peninsula. Jack had seen the trail of the 'Death March', had seen where General Wainwright had surrendered his starving army to the Japanese on Bataan.

Jack had visited Manila in 1965, a memorable trip to the hoary Army-Navy Club, and he wanted to go back. So, he recruited McNamara, Duvall and T. P. Burwell to accompany him. The four of them caught a helicopter to the embassy helicopter pad in Manila and then took rooms at the club, where members and their wives had listened to the Army-Navy game on the eve of Pearl Harbor. There they changed into bathing suits and drank gin gimlets around the pool, ogling and being ogled by the young ex-pat wives who lounged there. Jack eventually snagged a bikini-clad young one and went to his room, to which she soon followed him. The rest of them sweated against the canvas-clad loungers, ate burgers hot off the grill, drank more gin gimlets, smoked and watched Jack's triumphant return.

Stumbling drunk, they showered and began walking to the International Club, a sprawling complex of white, colonial era buildings with a polo field.

The road was filled with potholes, and they wobbled drunkenly in and out of them and occasionally fell, at which the others laughed until they fell also. At the club, they tried to pick up round-eyed women, but even Jack failed, so they went on to a whore house and drank some more and smoked more cigarettes and danced with the bar girls.

That night, after a few more drinks in the Bachelor's Bar there at the Army-Navy Club—women were admitted only on New Year's Eve—they stowed away on an admiral's 'barge' and rode down to Cavite, where Jack, years before, had gone. One of his shipmates, a lieutenant commander named Herb Jackson, had been stationed there and had bought a bar for his girlfriend. Jack thought Herb might be retired now and living there.

And he was. Herb Jackson greeted Jack warmly and ordered drinks on the house for the four of them. Once they were settled at a table with girls, Jack went to the rest room, and he saw a bene'—pronounced 'Benny'—boy pissing into a toilet over which he squatted like a girl. She—he—was indistinguishable from the other bar girls, and it scared Jack, because he was afraid that he might end up in bed with a Benny boy sometime. Strangely, Jack observed that most of the Filipino men kept one long fingernail that they used for god-knows-what. The next morning the four of them stood on the seawall and drank cold San Miguel beer and smoked cigarettes, blowing the smoke into a freshening breeze off the bay, while Jack wished for Melanie and an autumn day at Chapel Hill.

Back in 'Pubic Bay', as they called it, Olongapo, which he had never liked particularly—Hong Kong was his favorite port—beckoned from just beyond the 'Shit River'. It was a sewer that emptied the town of its monkey-meat-laden effluence, and into which small boys dived for quarters thrown from the bridge by sailors coming and going into the town across the bridge over the miasmal, turgid waters of the Shit River below.

Bars lined the dusty streets, and hucksters courted the sailors to come in to buy tea drinks for the bar girls. The thick warm air of southern Luzon held them in its vice-like grip. Vendors sold smoked monkey meat on sticks in front of the bars, and the execrable smell of it filled the air. The sailors had termed it monkey meat decades ago, but no one really knew what it was. At the Zanzibar, Jack's preferred officers' bar from his Princeton days, girls stood out front, beckoning them like Homeric sirens. Among them he had recognized the first one he had slept with back in the autumn of 1964. She had aged twenty years in four, and it scared him, maybe because in her face he saw his past and his present, and he didn't like what he saw. So, he moved on.

Jack found the bar from which he had pulled his last piece of Filipino ass in 1966, when he left the Princeton to teach at OCS. She was a beautiful girl, tall for a Filipino, because she was part Spanish, with the requisite beautiful Filipino olive skin, black hair and beautiful, dark eyes. She was, however, not a particularly good lay—she seemed indifferent to him—and he was glad to be shed of her when it was over, and he returned to the ship. Later, he would learn from his Princeton friend Eldon Bridges that she had given Eldon's friend, Haden 'Bugsy' Moran, the clap.

T. P. Burwell was a penguin-shaped man, whose face shone as though it had been worked over with an emery stick. He sported a high cowlick that rose like Everest abruptly out of his forehead, and his Irish eyes were as blue as cheap five-and-dime marbles. The second night, five of them had dinner at the Officers' Club, and three of them left Jack and Bill Stockwell dancing with Navy nurses from the big hospital set on the side of a high escarpment that overlooked the entrance to Subic Bay. The three junior officers—two were married—walked in the cooling twilight across the numbingly noxious smell that overhung the Shit River and on the town side, caught a pink jeepney—a World War II jeep converted into a taxi by attaching a canvas top to it—down to one of the officers' bars that stippled the main street. There, T. P., an Olongapo virgin, quickly hooked up with a beautiful bar girl and headed for her house off Main Street in a barrio filled with stick houses and the fetid smells of the dank town.

Liam McNamara, who was married, hooked up with a whore and headed to his girl's house, about a block from T. P.'s. He began doing his business when all of sudden he heard the keening wail of T. P. Burwell in acute distress. McNamara finished his business, gave the girl twenty pesos—about four dollars—and walked out into the malodorous air. There stood T. P., tucking in his shirt and reconstituting his civilian ensemble. "What the fuck happened, T. P.?" Liam McNamara asked.

"She's…he's a man," Burwell stammered.

"What the fuck? How? It looked like a woman. What the fuck?"

"That's what I want to know. Good god from Galveston. I almost threw up. Jesus."

Later, when word reached the wardroom of the Black, the XO told them of the bene' boys. "They are cross-dressers. There's a bar in San Francisco named Pinocchio's where all of the girls are men, and I'll be damned if you can tell the difference. You got screwed, blued and tattooed Mr. Burwell and I will guaran-damn-tee you that you will never forget your first whore in the P.I."

"Well, I didn't screw him but I did kiss him. Jesus. I've been spitting ever since. That's my last Filipino bar girl. I swear, holy Jesus, I swear holy Mary, mother of God. Nevermore."

They rented golf clubs and played at the Navy golf course, sweating heavily and then taking refuge from the rain in small shelters spread judiciously about the course. Afterward, Jack and his men sat in the unairconditioned bar and had drinks. They listened to the rain pounding on the tin roof and felt the cool air from the great ceiling fans circling overhead. He told them about William Faulkner in Oxford, how he had seen him once—only once—because Faulkner had become writer-in-residence at the University of Virginia. He told them about the *Rose for Emily* house, and about Benjy behind an iron fence and Faulkner as a boy walking by and later making him the main character in *The Sound and the Fury*.

Nights they went to the Cubi Point—a naval air station adjacent to the Subic Bay surface Navy base—Officers' Club. It sat upon a high outcropping of the mountains that surrounded Subic Bay, and it, too, was not air-conditioned. They drank there and felt a strong breeze off the bay through the screens that lined the bayside wall and watched the Phantom jets take off against the azure monsoon haze that enveloped the mountains, their afterburners orange and red against the darkening sky.

It had all been so new and so special when Jack had first seen it back in 1964, but now it was just old and past, and to Jack it meant nothing, except it was where he didn't want to be. He wanted to go home, go back to Melanie, go to law school, or get her to come out to Japan and marry him. But he couldn't, couldn't resign, couldn't go anywhere. He had two years to do, and trouble—deep shit trouble—lay on his horizon, although he didn't know it. Not yet, anyway.

So, in Subic Bay, he made up his mind and wrote to Melanie: Melanie: I love you more than anything in the world, and I want to marry you. Will you come to Japan and marry me? I can get us a place to live, and we can be together when I'm in port. And when the ship visits these other ports—like

Hong Kong, Subic Bay in the Philippines, Taipei in Taiwan and maybe even Bangkok, you can fly down and meet me, and you and I can be together. Please come marry me. I love you, and I want to spend the rest of my life with you. Jack

Tet

On the last day of January 1968, they received word that there had been an attack by North Vietnamese regulars and the Viet Cong over almost all South Vietnam. In history, this widespread attack would become known as the 'The Tet Offensive', because it began on the Lunar New Year, a shut-down holiday in Vietnam. Zumwalt, in Saigon, contacted the Seventh Fleet, and they ordered the Black River to return to Vietnam, specifically to a place called Hue—pronounced 'whay'—where the insurgents were sowing chaos and havoc among the few allied forces fighting there and were killing civilians all over the city. The Black was to go up the Perfume River, which ran from west to east and divided the city into northern and southern parts, with the 'new' city on one side and the 'old' city on the other. The old city was a hoary old bastion that dated back hundreds of years, and its lynchpin was the ancient citadel, with its outer wall over a yard thick and over five yards high. Behind the outer wall there was an inner wall, and the two walls created a formidable obstacle for anyone trying to take the citadel. The Black's mission was to support the Marines, who were attempting to retake the citadel from the North Vietnamese who had swarmed into it. The Black was not, however, to destroy the old city, an order of dubious efficacy calling for restraint. In other words, the Black was to fight with only one hand.

But there was another problem, far more serious. It was a matter of survival. Bill Stockwell had taken the little ship up the Saigon River a few months before, and it had taken a recoilless rifle round across the deck. Two feet lower, and the Black would have entered the Naval Archive of dead ships. They could expect more on the Perfume River.

Stockwell consulted his officers about the problem. "Any ideas?" he asked.

There was silence.

"Listen. I don't want to get this ship blown to hell and back. We need something to protect us. Think, guys."

Jack, who had two years of Army ROTC under his belt, thought. And he remembered. Sandbags. Sandbags would knock down most enemy fire that managed to penetrate the steel sides of the Black. "Sandbags," he said.

Stockwell jerked his head toward Jack. "Yes," he said, "that'd work. But where are we going to get sandbags?"

"I know," T. P. 'Benny' Burwell said. "If we can find empty bags, we can fill them with sand off the sand dunes on the beach. Pull the ship in close to the beach and use a mike boat to ferry the filled bags to us. We can get the base to hire Filipinos to fill the bags on the beach and put them on the mike boat and then our men can form a line and take them below and stack them against the sides."

"Yeah," Liam McNamara said. "Kind of like a rocket loadout. Form a line and pass the sacks to the hatches and down and then stack 'em against the bulkheads. That'd work."

They found the empty sacks with Marines who were assigned to guard the perimeter of the airfield at Cubi Point. The rest of it worked like a charm, and after two days of loading, they secured. The bulkheads were covered with sandbags, and the Black was ready for hell on the Perfume River. And it would be just that: hell.

It took another two days for the Black to chug across the South China Sea to the mouth of the Perfume River. On the way, they set up two large grills made out of oil drums, and the officers cooked hamburgers and steaks for the crew. It was one of the crew's favorite meals, and they loved that the officers did it. Bill Stockwell ordered them to switch into shorts and tee shirts, which they also loved. Morale was high. It would need to be high for what awaited them up the Perfume River.

They arrived on February 4, 1968. The Battle of Hue was in full flower. As Ecclesiastes had said over 2000 years before, it was a time for war, and 80,000 North Vietnamese regulars and Viet Cong insurgents had brought that war to—among other places—Vietnam's ancient and pseudo-sacred capital city. The captain ordered them to hoist the combat ensign, an oversized and tattered American flag that had seen extensive combat and was their good luck charm. It rose into the tropical sunlight and snapped in the wind.

The wardroom received a briefing from a swift boat—they had already been involved in combat around the citadel—squadron commander, and Jack had a brief visit with one of the swift boat commanders, his friend, Eldon

Bridges, from Jack's Princeton days. The fighting, Eldon said, was intense, with the enemy using large-caliber machine guns and the Black's old nemesis, recoilless rifle fire, to rake and drive off the Navy. "They will fucking blow you to that great Navy graveyard in the sky if you aren't careful. They are tough, tenacious soldiers and they are not afraid of anything you got. Even those damn rockets."

Then Jack, who had read a Navy publication entitled 'Sailings'—it gave information about every port in the world—navigated the Black upriver to the city, and a Marine forward artillery observer began directing their fire. They fired non-stop over the next six days until they ran out of rockets, and then they fired intermittently with their five-inch gun before heading back downriver and down the coast to Cam Ranh Bay. It was another rocket loadout in the midday sun and heat. The men humped the rockets into the racks below, just as they had the sandbags, and then it was back up the coast to the Perfume River.

Along the way, Jack fired an M-1 rifle at the war detritus that floated by them. As he fired, remembered a squirrel hunt in the Yazoo-Mississippi Delta in the autumn of '63, when a lazy mist rolled off the sluggish sloughs, and the sun rose, luminous through the already-skeletal cypress trees that rose spectrally from the water that defined the forest on three sides. The sun shone through the mist, limning the diaphanous vivid flecks that seemed to float in the old-growth forest. Up above, with the sunrise, large red fox squirrels began moving in the serried trees, and the four hunters shot them so that the beautiful fox-red creatures fell into the dead leaves that carpeted the forest floor. Later, that afternoon, Jack had watched the first game of the 1963 World Series between his beloved Yankees and the Los Angeles Dodgers. Sandy Koufax shut the Yankees down—skunked them—and Jack was saddened by the loss.

They started up the Perfume River, but this time they had received word that the banks were crawling with Viet Cong, so they opened up with two forty-millimeter pom-pom guns as they went upstream and took out any potential hostile fire. Upon arrival, a Marine major came aboard. His name was Pete Manning, and he was from Kentucky.

"We need something unusual from you this time: direct fire on the citadel walls to blow a hole we can go through. Goin' through the gates is like running through the fires of hell. It needs to be with the rockets because it needs to be fast so they can't move troops around in there. And it needs to be directed at the base of the walls so they'll collapse. Can you do that?"

"The problem we're gonna have," Liam McNamara said, "is getting the rockets aimed low enough to blast through the lower half of the walls. I've looked as those walls and they are formidable. I think we've got the firepower to do it if we could just get the rockets aimed lower. The launchers are locked so they won't fire lower than ten degrees above level so they won't hit the lifeline that runs along the edge of the deck."

"Give me a minute," Jack said. He paged Wallis to the gun deck. "Wallis, let me ask you something. We need to get these launchers aimed slightly—maybe five degrees—below level to hit the bottom of the walls and collapse them. Can you do it?"

"I don't know, sir. There's a locking device on each one that prevents you from firing too low and hitting the lifeline and stanchions that hold it."

"Well, can you undo the locking pin?"

"I can try, XO. Let me see what I can do. And if it works, we'll have to take down the steel posts that hold the wire that runs around the main deck and then the wire itself."

"Good. We can get the lifeline down but see what you can do with the locking device first. I'll be in the wardroom with this Marine major we got aboard. This is a pretty big deal and we need to help him if we can. Come get me when you figure it out—one way or the other."

Jack went back to the wardroom. "I got my expert working on it, Captain. Let's give him some time to see if he can unlock the locking devices."

"Great, XO. Good work. I'll keep my fingers crossed."

They brought in ice cream, which the major had not seen in weeks, and ate it, then chased it down with hot Navy coffee, and they smoked cigarettes, which were good after the ice cream and with the hot coffee. Major Manning did not smoke cigarettes, so the captain gave him one of his good cigars and he puffed on that. Then Wallis knocked, and Jack went out into the passageway.

"We—I—can do it, sir. It's tricky but I'm pretty sure I can pull it off. The problem is going to be getting the locking pin back in. I think I can but I haven't tried that. You want me to get on it, XO?"

"Yeah. Do only the starboard-side. We'll figure out reinstalling the locking pin when we get to it. Get 'em unlocked Wallis. Good work. And tell the Chief Bosun to get the lifeline on the starboard-side down."

Inside, Jack said, "We can do it, Captain."

"That's great, XO. Okay, gentleman, let's go to work."

That evening, Wallis pulled the out the locking pins, and the deck apes took down the lifeline and stanchions on the starboard-side. Then, the next morning at daybreak, they opened up on the base of the citadel walls. Six salvos from four launchers firing twelve-inch rockets slammed into the outer wall, and it collapsed. Then they fired into the inner wall and opened a gaping hole in it. The Marines poured in through the openings, and, for the insurgents in the citadel, church was just about out. For its work, the Black received a nomination for a Presidential Unit Citation that it would not receive. The admiral commanding the Seventh Fleet posited that they were just doing what they were supposed to do. Paul Sessums noted that it was easy for him to say that, tucked away on his cruiser in Subic Bay.

On March 2, 1968 came the last firefight, on the north side of the city, where the Marines were pushing the remaining insurgents out and back into the jungle. The XO and Liam McNamara had worked out a system in which the four starboard-side launchers, their pins removed, fired directly—line-of-sight—into the city, and the port rockets, still with their pins, fired indirectly on targets out-of-sight. That system required rotating the ship to bring either the portside or starboard-side launchers into play and rotating fast. On March 2, they were firing indirectly, when an onslaught of machine-gun and recoilless rifle fire slammed into them like a typhoon.

The gunfire peppered the ship's port side, where the pinned launchers couldn't get low enough to fire directly and take on the insurgents, so the captain instructed the OOD, Hinky Henderson, to rotate the ship so as to put the starboard-side direct fire launchers in a position to fire. As the Black rotated, she caught hell from the enemy weapons ashore. Recoilless rifle fire slammed into her sides and went off against the sandbags, blowing gaping holes in the Black's steel sides and knocking down the contiguous sandbags, and, with the concussion from the explosions against the Black's sides, sailors manning the rocket launchers went down. Machine-gun fire raked the bridge and pilot house, ricocheted off the metal sides, put the men on the bridge on the deck.

The XO ordered the forward and aft forty millimeters to open up and suppress the insurgent fire, and they did. But in the meantime, a recoilless rifle shell exploded as it entered the bridge and another in the pilot house below. The bridge filled with brains and blood and bone fragments and intestines.

Jack and Stockwell crouched behind the steel bulkheads, and Jack wondered how he had gone from Melanie and Chapel Hill to this conflagration at Hue. Liam McNamara leaned against a bulkhead on the other side of the bridge, wounded and bleeding hard. They continued rotating until they had brought the starboard launchers to bear, and they opened up, and chewed up the jungle along the river. The firing ceased, and the Black headed downriver.

The recoilless rifle rounds took out a helmsman in the pilot house, hit the boatswain of the watch, killed a quartermaster on the port compass, and several of them, including Jack, the Captain and Liam McNamara, had taken metal splinters from a recoilless rifle shell that exploded when it hit the fire control tower at the aft part of the bridge. All of them would receive purple hearts.

It was now time to head for Yokosuka for repairs. They met an underway replenishment ship—called an 'unrep' ship—outside the mouth of the river, and in heavy seas, Jack drove the Black and kept her alongside the unrep ship until the Black's fuel tanks were topped off with the diesel fuel that powered the two engines. Then it was north for home. But first, a stop in Hong Kong for them to lick their wounds and salve their bodies with booze.

Bill Stockwell, who would receive a silver star, put Jack in for a bronze star with a combat 'V' for valor and the other officers in for Navy commendation medals, also with Combat Vs. Those medals would come back to haunt the officers of the Black River at a day that would not be long in coming.

A Letter from Melanie

The letter came aboard with the mail from the unrep ship. It was from Melanie. With excitement, Jack opened the letter. He was anything but confident that she would take him up on his offer. If she would—a big *if*—he would buy her the ticket, and she would come, and they would get married.

She wrote:

Dear Jack: I got your letter and yes, my love. I will absolutely come out and marry you. I love you so much. Is it hard to get married out there? Do you know how to do it? Let me finish my masters coursework spring semester, and I'll do my dissertation in June and July and come out in August. We can work out the exact dates later.

Here, anti-war demonstrations are almost constant. They sit in at the post office where the recruiting offices are and they march around campus chanting, "Hell no. We won't go." Guys are burning their draft cards right and left. I don't know what will happen to them if they get drafted and don't go. I guess they will go to jail or maybe to Canada, which is what some of them have done.

Well, that's about it from Carolina land except to say that right now all I care about is marrying you and having you once again. I love you so much, Melanie.

He wrote her back:

Dearest Melanie:

Thank god. I was so afraid that I had lost you, and I am thrilled that you will come out here and marry me. I have absolutely been scared to death that I would never see you again, but yes, summer's fine, and I will make arrangements for the marriage. I don't know what we have to do, but I will find out and be ready to go when you arrive. I'll have to coordinate your timing with the Black's schedule, but that shouldn't be much of a problem. Just looking ahead and based on the schedule we have followed in the past, we should be back during the summer. I will also get us a place to live out 'on the economy' as they say when you live off the base. I think you will love it out here, and there is so much for us to see and do. I can take leave, and we can travel all over Japan, and when we go into Subic Bay in the Philippines, you can fly down there and meet me, and we can go to Manila and Baguio, which is up in the mountains and cool, both weather-wise and otherwise. It is an international sort of place, with great restaurants and military housing that you rent for the days you want to be there. We can stay there and eat and drink and make love and just have each other. I can think of nothing that I would love more than just being with you and loving you, which I do, so much.

Jack

Chapter Seven
Hong Kong

Because of her size—small—the Black was able to tie up at a small pier near Government House, a white two-story colonial building fronted by the Union Jack and a cricket field. Jack conned her in and he splintered the old wooden pier, as he had done several times to the pier in Cam Ranh Bay. He still lacked the requisite depth perception and invariably came in high and hard, like an overthrown fastball.

That first night in Hong Kong, the wardroom dined together at Jimmie's Kitchen, which had lived in the XO's memory as one of the finest restaurants he had ever experienced. Now with his new shipmates, he drank scotch and wine and ate escargot and a filet until, with the Drambuie, he was sick, and then he threw up—accompanied by stupefying diarrhea—in the men's room, where two Chinese attendants marveled at his prodigious capacity for both.

On the second night, the Black's officers picked up Chinese whores in a bar and took them to a cheap hotel on the Kowloon side that the girls recommended. Jack declined and stayed on the ship to watch 'Funny Girl' with Barbra Streisand. Later, they told him that T. P. Burwell had run out of money and paid his girl only five Hong Kong dollars. The going rate was fifteen—three dollars American. She took the money and looked at it for a long five or ten seconds then placed it in her pocket and came up from her right side with an openhanded slap that rattled T. P.'s brain down to his toes. His left cheek inflamed, he grabbed for her, but she kicked him in the shin with her pointed shoes. He yowled, and she ran. Jason Cohen and Paul Sessums fared better, so it was a split decision for the men of the Black River wardroom.

After four days, they fought their way out of Hong Kong harbor through heavy fog and even heavier boat traffic, sounding the ship's horn and easing ahead at a knot or two while Bill Stockwell sat quietly watching his expert musicians play in the Black's ship-handling orchestra. Then it was open sea and around the China horn and into the Taiwan Straits, where they caught the Kurashia, also known as the Black Current—some also called it the Japan Current—and were swept north at fifteen knots, three above the Black's top speed.

Jack went to the pilot house and watched the helmsman steer. "Let me try that, Barnes," he said after watching. He took the wheel and steered while Barnes advised him on the finer points of steering. Then Jack called up to the bridge. "Mr. Burwell, I want to maneuver some. Zigzag along our course just to see how she handles. Call the captain and tell him what we're going to do. He won't care. Then give me orders to steady up on new courses at forty-five-degree angles off base course for three minutes, say. Going back and forth we can maintain our course north."

The captain, indeed, didn't care, and they began the maneuvers. Barnes advised Jack exactly what to do: how to come right with standard-rudder, how to watch the compass as she turned and then 'meet her'—turn the wheel to port standard-rudder to steady up on the new course. They maneuvered, and Jack got the feel of it, and he now understood how the Black responded: how long it took for her to start her turn after the command, and how long it took the helmsman to react. Jack loved it, and nights after he finished shooting stars, he would take a fifteen-minute turn at the wheel. A day out from Yokosuka, the engineering officer, Jason Cohen, appeared in Jack's door. He was occasionally called Harry for obvious reasons. Once Paul Sessums had seen him in the shower. "Why don't you take off your sweater, Harry?" he asked.

"What is it, Harry?" Jack asked.

"I'm embarrassed to say it but I've got the clap."

"Holy shit. Where and when?"

"Hong Kong. Showed up day before yesterday."

"Have you seen the corpsman?"

"No sir. I don't want anyone on board to know."

"Well, we'll be in at Yoko tomorrow. Then get your ass over to the base infirmary and get some treatment. Okay?"

"Yessir. Will do."

The next day, the Black River—bruised and battered—pulled into Yokosuka Harbor. Most of the rocket ships'—there were three others—staff from Comphibron Eleven awaited, and they applauded the men of the Black as Bill Stockwell pulled her alongside the pier into an offsetting wind that required the use of mike boats—controlled by the XO—to push the Black into the freshening north wind.

Melanie

Melanie had received Jack's second letter. She answered:

Dear Jack:

What a wonderful letter. I can think of nothing else but marrying you and coming out to Japan and just living there in a Japanese house with you. Thank you so much for asking me to be your wife.

I am involved here in a number of causes that interest me. You will be interested to know that Walter Cronkite, who usually supports the government, came out and said that the war is unwinnable. So did Robert Kennedy and Chet Huntley. Did you know about that horrible incident at My Lai. That did it for me. I think I have a moral imperative to fight the war effort, and I am going to do everything in my power to do that, but that doesn't make me love you less. I know you are just out there doing your duty, and I would guess that you probably don't support the war any more than I do.

I have decided to support Eugene McCarthy for president, and I think most college students do. He is the only candidate who opposes the war. I want to end that damn war and get us—and you—home after I come out there. But I doubt if it will end, because I don't see how we can win it. Tet convinced us all that it is unwinnable.

Incidentally, Joan Baez was here, and her concert was fabulous. She sang a lot of anti-war songs, and if I weren't converted before to the anti-war movement, I am now. Incidentally, Bob Dylan was badly hurt in a motorcycle accident. And back to the war, Martin Luther King has called for a rally in Washington to protest this damn war, and I am going up with a bunch from Chapel Hill. And one more thing: a guy named Rod McKuen has a new book out called 'Listen to the Warm'. You ought to read it. It will be good for your soul. It was for mine.

Please take care of yourself and know that I love you more than anything in the world.

Melanie

Chapter Eight
Yokosuka

It was the Ides of March, and they learned that day that Bill Stockwell was leaving the Black. His replacement was to be a Destroyer School classmate of his named Robert 'The Corkscrew' Cork: according to Bill Stockwell, a certifiably crazy man from Madison, Wisconsin. "I'll guarantee you this," Stockwell told the wardroom, "You have never seen anything or anyone like him. He's a holy damn terror."

Stockwell's words would prove prophetic. Cork was that and more. He arrived three days after they tied up and relieved Stockwell two days later, on March 20. Cork tore through the ship like a knife through warm butter, yelling, cursing and at times screaming madly at his crew. He was tall and well built, with thick black hair that he combed straight back into an oily pompadour and thick heavy eyebrows set hard against whiter-than-white skin that made his face look like that of a B-movie vampire. He wore his tailored uniform well, and he told the wardroom that he was going to have the ass of any officer who did not comply with his orders to a 'T'. And he then he turned to Jack. "That includes you, XO. Especially you." Cork then left the wardroom and from above came what was to be his characteristic slammed stateroom door.

Jack was stunned. Bill Stockwell had never said anything with even a hint of negativity to Jack at all, and he would have shot himself before he did it in front of the junior officers. "Well, I guess that tells me what my situation is," Jack told them. "I'm going to be just like one of you except maybe worse. But I guarantee you this: I'm going to do my best to be a buffer between him and you but I imagine that there is only so much that I can do, especially when you are alone with him on the bridge. Good luck, guys. Do your best and I will do my best to shield you from him."

In the end, it was worse than any of them could have imagined. Outraged at the medals that his officers had received—and that he didn't have—he took it out on them. His wife had not arrived yet, so Cork stayed on the ship each day from 0700 to 2000, ripping and snorting and giving the wardroom and the crew hell. He wanted a clean, shiny ship, wanted the men in dress uniforms day and night, wanted the wardroom in dress blues rather than working khaki and foul-weather jackets, and he wanted the XO to inspect the ship's messing and berthing spaces every day. Cork had graduated from Loyola, Chicago, and the XO reminded him of the 1962 NCAA tournament when the Mississippi state team had sneaked out of Starkville on a plane at night because of Mississippi's ban against playing sports against Blacks. The all-white state team had played the all-Black Loyola team, which had gone on to win the NCAA tournament. But Cork said, "Fuck that shit. I don't care about any of that crap."

Cork used wardroom meals as a vehicle for propounding criticism of his officers. Hinky Henderson was a pussy who didn't know shit about deck operations. Liam McNamara was a pussy for letting his subordinate Henderson get away with it. Paul Sessums was a milk toast and a 'whip sock' because he was Paul Sessums, and his manner was gentle, and he was soft-spoken. Dave Duvall was a teathead, because the galley, Duvall's responsibility, burned Cork's toast one morning. Jason Cohen was a snipe who didn't know enough about engineering to fill Cork's little finger. And the XO needed to ride them harder to make them do 'right'. The wardroom performance appraisals would remain for the duration a part of Cork's arsenal of personnel weapons.

Cork made Cockroach shine all of the officers' shoes—daily—whether they needed it or not. He made the XO rewrite the ship's instructions to comply with Cork's many predilections, eccentricities and phobias—no sideburns, no mustaches, no chin whiskers, two officers aboard at all times—and he made the wardroom stay aboard at night with him and watch movies that they had already seen. He put Liam McNamara in hack—keeping him from his wife and two children—for not wearing his blue uniform coat in the wardroom, and he put Paul Sessums in hack because his chief petty officer came aboard loud and drunk. "You pukes are going to learn to do it my way or you'll be spending a lot of time onboard this ship. Sessums, you skinny piece of shit, you got this problem with that chief because you've never asserted command and control of him. Now get cracking or you're gonna sit out Yokosuka."

But the XO was his favorite target. He had him paged every hour. The loudspeaker system crackled all day: "XO to the captain's cabin. XO to the wardroom. XO to the mess decks. XO to the forward berthing space. To the forward head. To the after head. XO. XO. XO." And it was all trivial shit, Jack thought. A dirty toilet. A rack not made properly. A coffee stain on the mess decks floor. On and on, the problems mounted. Finally, Cork sought and received permission to move the Black to an anchorage, where he put the entire ship in hack, except for him, and he used the ship's motor whaleboat to escape each night and return each morning. The men began calling him Bluto, like Popeye's nemesis, the quintessence of bullydom.

As he had said he would, Jack took the pounding for his JOs, but he had them correct the problems. He inspected the ship harder and harder, but always, there was something that the captain could find: a faint spot of dust on the underside of a table in the mess decks, a lavatory in the crew's head that did not sparkle, a sailor's rack that did not meet Officer Candidate School inspection standards.

He called Jack over the speaker system to report to his cabin. Jack was in the middle of his inspection of messing and berthing. He stopped and went there.

"XO, I've read this letter you wrote for me to sign on the combat action ribbon for these new guys who went through Rach Gia and Tet. It needs a comma there and another there. Do it over."

"Aye, Captain."

He turned to leave.

"There is something else. You are too easy on the JOs. I want you to crack down on them. Be a hard ass. Put the stick to them, not the carrot. Do you understand, XO?"

"Sir, my philosophy is that people react better to positive leadership than to negative leadership from someone who harps on their mistakes. I tell them in private what their mistakes are and praise them when they get it right. I think that makes them want to get it right for the praise, don't you?"

"Damn it, XO. You just don't get it, do you? You must be a pussy like Sessums and Henderson. Crack down on them. That's an order. Do it! Now!"

"Aye, aye sir."

"And there's one more thing. Goddamnit XO, are you aware that Mr. Henderson doesn't know shit from shinola about deck operations? Now that's your damn responsibility so get the hell on it and get his sorry ass straight. You understand?"

"Yessir, Captain. But I would be remiss if I didn't point out that Mr. Henderson reports to Mr. McNamara but if you want me to take direct responsibility for him I will."

"What the fuck, man? Can't you hear? Am I whispering or something? You goddam right I want you to take charge. It's just one more thing that you're not doing. So, get your ass in gear and get that creampuff piece of shit up to snuff. And in the meantime, put that sorry sonofabitch in hack."

"Aye, Sir. Will do."

"You goddam right you will do it. Now get your ass to it."

Cork smoked big, cheap cigars, and he filled the wardroom with a heavy cloud of putrid smoke that wiped out Jack's appetite. "Goddamit," Cork would shout. "If you pukes thought you killed Commies for Christ under Bill Stockwell, you're getting ready to find out how to really do that. I know more about gunnery than all of you put together and we're gonna eat those yellow bastards alive."

The Yokosuka Officers' Club Junior Officers' Dance

It was late March, but it was still cold and dreary, and it was a Wednesday night J.O. dance night at the O Club for the JO's. Jack and his JO's warmed up for it there with about three rounds of drinks, rolling the dice before each round to see who paid. It was not a big deal. The drinks were fifteen cents, and after months on the gunline, everyone was flush.

On the far wall from them, the one with stained-glass windows like a church, there was a fireplace, and the fire crackled with new unseasoned wood. Cigarette smoke filled the room and pooled at the ceiling like a bad hangover. Soft light from the chandeliers cast a viscous glow about the room, barely penetrating the almost-opaque haze that hung over the room.

In the next room, they could hear the band warming up: a tinny five-piece Japanese outfit that was playing 'Jack the Knife', and to which the early arrivals were doing various—and strange—dances, extant there as though trapped in some kind of a Yokosuka 1956 time-warp. Jack did not intend to go in. He was engaged now and could think of no one other than Melanie. But he drank, and as he drank, his resistance weakened, so he joined his JOs and went into the ballroom. There was no fire there, and it was a tenebrous, desultory place.

They took a table and ordered another round of drinks and lit cigarettes and exhaled smoke that rose into the warm ochre light. Jack had more drinks until he was a besotted mess. Two tables down the wall, there were two women, mature women, with wedding bands and big teats. The brunette was looking at Jack. She got up and came over to Jack.

"Hi, there," she said. "Want to dance?"

Jack looked the married woman over. She was of medium height and busty, with dark hair and incongruous blue eyes. What could he say? No? Send her back to her table, humiliated? No, he couldn't do that. "Yes," he said finally.

They did the boogaloo and then slow-danced. She held him close, and she told him that her husband was an officer on the USS Waddell, a destroyer home-ported there in Yokosuka, and they had been in Yokosuka only a couple of months when he sailed for the Vietnam gunline, where he had been the last four months. She told him that they had two children and lived out on the economy.

"And what about you?" she asked.

"I'm the executive officer of the Black River, a rocket ship. We just got back from the gunline down there. We fired all our rockets at Hue, where we took heavy hostile fire, and went to Hong Kong and then came home, to the extent this is home for any of us. Our ship's quarters are substandard, which is an understatement, so we're staying at the BOQ."

"Well, I want to know one thing," she said. "Where did you get those eyes?"

"From my mother, I guess. She has the bluest eyes I've ever seen."

"Well, yours are green. And I love your accent. It's the most southern accent I've ever heard. Where'd you get it?"

"I'm from Mississippi. Got it there, I guess. Where're you from?"

"Fairfax. Virginia. I've been gone from there a long time. I went out to San Diego when I finished college at Virginia Commonwealth. Met my husband there. We've been married eight years now."

He pegged her as thirtyish, five or so years older than he was.

She looked into his green eyes. It was the look of a sad, lonely woman. "You want to come home with me?" she asked.

No. I can't do that. I've got to be loyal to Melanie. I'll tell her no. And then he looked at her sad face and heard himself saying yes, that he would. Jack simply didn't want to hurt her feelings. He was too nice. And besides, Melanie would never know. They left together. Outside, in the cold, drizzly night, they caught a cab and rode out to Kamakura, where the big Buddha sat, and she paid off the sitter, and they had sex on a futon in her living room before an oil heater that strained to keep the room warm. Early the next morning, she gave him strong black coffee with lots of sugar, and he caught the first train of the morning back down to Yokosuka, enveloped in a cloud of cheap Japanese cigarette smoke and a cloud of guilt. It was a deadly combination—booze and sex—but he wouldn't do it again.

Or would he?

Cohen

The message came through on April Fool's Day. Cohen's family wanted him home for his grandmother's funeral.

He still had the clap.

"Jesus, XO. I can't go. What the fuck?"

"You're fucked. That's what. Whatta you want me to do?"

"Can you say I can't be spared?"

"Yeah. I can say that. But I have to clear it with the CO first, which means that I've got to tell him you've got clap."

"Oh, Jesus," Cohen moaned. "Oh, god. He'll have my ass in hack in less than a minute."

"Well, it's all I can do. I can't send a message like that without his permission."

"We've got to do it or I'll end up having to explain to my wife why I can't have sex with her."

"Can't you use a rubber?"

"I think she'd smell a rat, XO. She's on the pill and I haven't ever used a rubber."

Jack went to Cork, who called Cohen in and chewed on his ass for a while about how he was a stain on the Navy's honor, and he then granted Jack permission to send the message.

The reply came the next day. "You are ordered to send Ensign Cohen home ASAP. Strong Congressional interest."

"Oh, my god!" Cohen squealed. "Oh, my god! Oh Jesus! No!"

Cohen left that afternoon on a flight out of Tachikawa Air Force Base. Harry took with him a bottle of penicillin tablets and a jock strap to hold the discharge from his diseased pecker.

He never came back. They boxed up his gear and shipped it to his home in Gary, Indiana. The wardroom of the Black never heard of, or from, Cohen again and wondered occasionally what had been the outcome of his peculiar, and to their knowledge, unprecedented, recall home.

The grandmother's death reminded Jack of what he did not want to be reminded: his father's death in the Greene County hospital between his tour in Newport teaching at OCS and his entry into the University of North Carolina in the fall of 1967. They had found a mass on his lung the previous winter and operated unsuccessfully in December of 1966. Still, they assured Jack's mother that he had a good chance of beating the cancer through radiation and chemotherapy. *What a joke,* Jack now thought. The lung cancer had metastasized and then moved quickly into his brain. By that summer—the summer of '67—his father, a 200-pound man, weighed less than 100 and was permanently curled into a fetal position and in a permanent coma. He died in June, with the family surrounding him, and Jack wept. He still ached for the loss. His father had been his polar star, to whom Jack could always turn for direction. He would have advised Jack to go to law school. Jack missed him and his advice. He always would.

Two weeks after Cohen's ignominious departure, a shiny new engineering officer named Bob Tyson reported aboard. He was single, and he was dark and hairy like Jason Cohen and looked greasy and black like a snipe. Tyson had the shape of a prune, and his face was stippled with crimson pimples, which was highly unusual for a 23-year-old man, but the Zit—as he would be known—would prove to be a highly unusual man.

Another Letter from Melanie

Dear Jack:

Well, the most amazing thing happened. You've probably read about it by now. LBJ announced that he will not run for reelection. All of us who support

Eugene McCarthy are thrilled. We feel that this gives him a chance to win and to end this awful war. Robert Kennedy, of course, has entered the race, but I don't know about that, and Hubert Humphrey probably will, too.

Here, things are picking up with the anti-war protests. There are demonstrations almost daily down in front of the recruiting depot, as they call it. Some students have demonstrated against the draft in front of the ROTC building, but I don't see much point in that. They don't have anything to do with the draft.

Carolina had a good basketball team and went to the finals of the NCAA tournament. Unfortunately, they had to play against UCLA in the finals, and UCLA was undefeated and never loses. They didn't lose this time either. UCLA has a player named Lew Alcindor. You may have heard of him. He seven feet and two inches tall and is virtually unstoppable. He just killed us. We have no one that size, and they beat us by over twenty points. Oh well, there is always next year.

I miss you so much, Jack, and I'm so excited about coming to Japan and marrying you. Thank you so much for asking me to share my life with you, and you your life with me.

I am so excited.

With love,
Melanie

The Admiral's Daughter

He met her at the Officers' Club in early April. She was with some Navy nurses whom T. P. invited to join them at Jack's table. Her name was Amanda Brown, and she was 28 years old and teaching at what they called Yoko High, the military high school in Yokohama. Her father was a Vice-Admiral and commander of the Yokosuka Navy Base, and they lived on a high hill overlooking Yokosuka Harbor. A few days after the dance, she called him on the Black River and invited him for drinks and dinner at the admiral's quarters. He had never been to an admiral's quarters, and so he accepted and went there on an unseasonably cold April night.

After the horrors of meals with Cork, the gathering at the admiral's house seemed absolutely loosey-goosey. They sat in a living room with a crackling fire maintained by one of the three Filipino stewards who serviced the family. Amanda had picked up the latest California styles—a blue miniskirt cut up almost to her buttocks and a magenta blouse with a collar so long that the points hit her shoulders. She wore knee-high shiny white boots like Jack had never seen. Amanda had hazel eyes and pretty legs and a good body. She reminded him of a girl he had once loved in Long Beach named Karen Freese, whom he had left behind when he drove out of there in his green MGB and headed east across the country to Newport, where he quickly moved on, without explanation or even so much as a letter after promising her that he would be in touch. Now, with this reminder, he thought of her, as he did for every one of them he had left behind.

Jack drank his winter drink, scotch and water, and smoked and watched the fire hiss and sizzle, flashing luminously off the darkly paneled lacquered walls of the living room. Admiral Brown was an aviator and had gone through Pensacola flight training in 1940, when Jack's father had been stationed there at Fort Barrancas in the Coastal Artillery branch of the Army. Jack was born there six days after Pearl Harbor, but Admiral Brown was long gone to San Diego by then.

"Jack, I understand that you were at Hue for Tet and that you got a purple heart. Is that right?"

"Yessir. It wasn't much of a wound but I guess it counts no matter how insignificant it is."

"Yes, it does. I got mine at the Marianas Turkey Shoot in forty-four. It was just a piece of steel off my plane's cockpit that caught me in the face and gave me a nice razor cut. They all count."

Jack studied the admiral. He was about Jack's height and slightly stooped, with thinning brown hair that was receding, and he had a cigarette in his hand. And a drink, both constantly. "I've read about that, Admiral Brown. There were several officers on the Princeton who had been there."

"You know, Jack, the predecessor ship to your Princeton was sunk there. The skipper lost a leg but they gave him another carrier. He served out the war on her. He was the last one-legged skipper in the Navy. It's quite a story."

"I knew she was sunk there but I didn't know about the skipper."

"Yep, that's the story. There's a movie: 'In Harm's Way', with John Wayne. I understand that it's based on that guy. In the movie, Wayne loses a leg, and Admiral Nimitz tells him that he's going to get a new leg and a new ship and go all the way to Tokyo with the fleet. Great movie. I saw it at the Officers' Club a few years ago. Really enjoyed it."

They drank. And they drank. And they drank.

Jack, now on the dull edge of drunk, took Amanda to the Officers' Club that night. They watched a movie—The 'Thomas Crown Affair'—and he drank more after dinner than he had before dinner. Later, in his MGB, he, dead drunk, took her to the top of one of the hills overlooking the base and had sex. Like Bob Tyson in Hong Kong, he did not use a rubber, but unlike Harry, he felt guilt again: enormous, all-enveloping guilt over his unfaithfulness to Melanie. And he hurt because of it. And once again, he vowed that he would not do it again. Amanda Brown would be a one-night stand. He would stay away from her. From all women. Jack would wait for summer and Melanie. He would stay clean.

Dinner with the Chiefs

On the Black, the days ground on, noisy and dusty from sanding off the paint on the Black's steel hull. The Japanese repair facility patched up the shell holes they had taken at Hue, restored the bridge and rebuilt the pilot house. In the meantime, the chief petty officers—the snipe, Chief Harold Ingold; Jack's assistant navigator, Chief Bart Baucom, and the chief boatswain's mate, Chief Vincent Majors—invited the officers to join them at the CPO Club for drinks and dinner. Jack was reluctant: he had learned on the Princeton that it was wise to maintain a gulf between officers and enlisted, and that officers and enlisted men and booze did not mix well, but Cork insisted that they go, so on a chilly April evening, with the cherry trees in bloom and the sea hawks swooping low over Yokosuka Harbor, they joined the chiefs for drinks and dinner. The problem was the drinks.

The chiefs drank straight whiskey out of shot glasses and chased it with beer—boilermakers—before and through dinner and then brought on more drinks after dinner. Cork was his usual self: salty, acerbic and at times, insulting. Finally, Chief Baucom, now drunk, had heard enough. He began by calling Cork a fucking asshole and then continued with various epithets that described Cork's demeanor and personality. Baucom stood and showed how Cork would be when the firing started: crouching and shaking and squealing like a little pig. Finally, the XO had heard enough.

"That's it, Chief Baucom. Enough. Sit down and shut up or get the hell out of here before I write you up for insubordination."

Baucom came across the table with glasses and plates crashing and grabbed Jack by the neck and slammed him over backward in the chair, so that Jack's head crashed into the floor. "Goddamn you summa-fuckin'-bitch I'll beat hell out of you."

Cork and McNamara pulled him off, and the other two chiefs apologized and took him back to the ship. The next day Baucom came to the XO's cabin and apologized. "I don't feel I can serve in the Black anymore, XO. I'm puttin' in for a transfer."

"You can put in for a transfer all you want, Chief Baucom, but I'm going to keep your sorry ass here and I'm gonna court-martial you. You have bought the farm on this one. Gross insubordination and an assault on an officer. You're dead. At a minimum, you'll get busted, and if I have my way it'll be six, six and a kick."

Baucom broke into tears. "Oh, XO, this is all I got. I got no family. I got no skills other than navigation and what the hell am I gonna do with that? Please XO. Please."

Jack dismissed the chief and convened a special court martial. They busted him two grades to second-class petty office, sentenced him to thirty days in the brig and fined him two months' pay but did not kick him out of the service. A day later, new Quartermaster Second Class Baucom began thirty days in the brig. Because he had assaulted an officer, physical punishment was the prescribed regimen. They used a combination of physical exercise beyond endurance and sleep deprivation, and they beat him with fists and a rubber hose.

Baucom ran continuously around a yard, and after a few laps, as a heavy smoker, he was slammed, but the Marines picked him up and punched him a few times and made him keep going. They also made him do pushups until he couldn't, then they punched him some more and made him start over. When he dropped, they kicked him silly. Baucom broke on his fifth day and sat in his cell crying. The Marines gathered to laugh at him. "Hell, Baucom," the Gunny said. "You ain't seen nothin' yet. Save your fuckin' tears. We're just gettin' started with your sorry ass. Douse him down, boys."

They put a fire hose on him and drove him into a corner where he crouched, crying. "Oh god, please stop. Please stop."

But there was—and would be—no mercy, and 'the treatment', as they called it, continued day and night. Exercise. Beatings and the hose, around the clock.

Cork once again put the entire ship in hack because, strangely, of Baucom's transgression, although he found an excuse in the cleanliness of the ship. The ship's company was outraged. They began calling him Bluto Corkscrew, and, when he did something back, they said that the CO had corkscrewed them. They began planning their revenge. It would not be long in coming.

Chapter Nine
The Second Cruise

They left Yokosuka on May 2 for Cam Ranh Bay, and the officers' wives came aboard to say goodbye. The wives left the ship early, careful to precede Elizabeth Cork, because Captain Cork had ordered the wardroom to get their wives and girlfriends off the ship before his wife departed. It was but one more of his strange predilections.

The first adventure with their new CO came when he got the Black underway, first moving her from the pier. A slight breeze would move her, because of her small draft and high profile. He was a destroyer driver and thus accustomed to quick responses from the ship and little drift from the wind. The Black, however, was different. This day there was more than a breeze: there was a steady wind that pushed her around like a paper sailboat on a windy day.

Cork was improvident, at best. He got her stern out safely, took in line three, then rammed her back at full. He would show these idiot JO's. He was a destroyer man, and destroyer men were the best ship handlers in the world.

The Black roared backward. And backward. And farther backward. A nest of LSTs loomed larger and larger behind her. On Cork went. Liam McNamara used the sound-powered phone to order the deck apes to put out bumper pads on the Black's stern. Finally, Cork ordered all ahead full. It was too late. The Black rammed into an LST, upon whose deck sailors watched in amazement. And they were yelling. Who was the madman driving that tub of shit?

Finally, the Black's engines dug in, and she went forward, but again too fast. Cork came hard right. Hard right was too far right. His speed was too much. The Black headed for another nest, this time, a nest of destroyers. Jack looked at him in horror. Cork had frozen, just like Jack had when he first took her in at Cam Ranh Bay. Cork gritted his teeth. He was tight-jawed, and the veins in his neck protruded like pipes. He looked ahead grimly.

"Captain," Jack shouted, "may I take the conn?"

There was nothing.

"Captain! May I take the conn?"

Finally, Cork answered, "Goddamit, XO. Hell no. Let Mr. McNamara have it." Then he turned and walked away, went down the ladder and went into his stateroom. His door slammed. On the bridge, there was a stunned silence. Then Liam McNamara took the conn, reversed his engines full emergency, got the Black on Jack's recommended course, and headed out to the maritime madness of Tokyo Bay.

The Tokyo Expressway

The Black River drove south down the Tokyo Bay freeway, filled with everything from junks and sampans to enormous oil tankers and gargantuan freighters, one of which could have fit eight Black Rivers in its hold. Cork heard the engines humming and knew that they were clear of the harbor and thus out of harm's way. He returned to the bridge, sat in his chair morosely, and lit a cigar. It was the usual Tokyo Bay chaos. Merchant ships raced by them, cut in front of the Black River, came at them from four quarters. Some came straight at them in a game of nautical chicken.

There were, of course, rules of the road that governed all of these situations, but the ships in Tokyo Bay seemed to be driven by captains who didn't know the rules existed, or didn't care. It was a cataclysmic nautical free-for-all, and it was as though the Black was the new kid in the hall with a 'kick me' sign on its stern. As they proceeded due south on a course of 180 degrees, the traffic thickened, and more of them came at the small ship from all angles, from all sides, at all speeds, and each close encounter sent Cork into screaming fits. He raced from side to side on the bridge, yelling and cursing, screaming and shaking his fist at other ships, at his officer-of-the-deck, Liam McNamara, and at the helmsman below in the pilot's house.

So, as Cork spewed streams of gratuitous invective, Jack fed course and speed recommendations to Liam McNamara, and Paul Sessums, in CIC fed solutions to the problems that the merchant ships were causing. "Contact at 225, 800 yards. He'll pass astern of us. No problem. Recommend maintain course and speed." The bridge's sound-powered phone operator relayed the information to Liam McNamara, who said, "Very well," and went on.

But not very far. "What the goddamn hell did that teathead say?"

"He said to maintain course and speed, sir."

"What the fuckin' shit? That goddamn puke. Come left to new course one-three-five, Mr. McNamara. We got to dodge that sonofabitch that's comin' on from two two five."

"Sir, we're the burdened ship. He's going to pass astern of us. We should, under the rules of the road, maintain course and speed."

"I don't give a good goddam about the fuckin' rules of the road. Come left to one-three-five. Now!"

McNamara said, "Aye, sir," and came left. The ship at two two five began sounding his horn, as if to say, "What the hell?"

Cork ignored him and began given commands. Come right to one eight zero, left to zero nine zero, right to two two zero, random, nonsensical, dangerous commands.

"Captain," Jack said, "a good way to do this is to go two-thirds, maintain our course, and sound the horn once a minute. All of these small craft will get out of our way and we can maneuver in accordance with the rules of the road to avoid the big boys. It always works out."

"Is that the way Bill Stockwell did it?" Cork asked.

Jack said it was.

"Well, I don't give a fat fuck what Bill Stockwell did. This is my ship now and we're gonna do it my way. Do you understand, XO?"

Jack said that he did understand, and they moved on, dodging and dancing like Sugar Ray Robinson.

It went on like this until they finally cleared Tokyo Bay, and the traffic thinned out to a more manageable consistency.

They sailed on, toward the unknown, under the command of a shouting madman, screaming obscenities and, as he called it, 'busting JO ass'. Jack's ass took a few bruises, as well.

In the wardroom, Cork's explosions punctuated every meal that he took there. Mercifully, he took some of the meals in his stateroom, served by Delos Reyes. When Cork did dine in the wardroom, the JO's sat implacably, awaiting the next explosion. Then, after a suitable time, they began asking to be excused, skulking out of the wardroom and disappearing into the not-so-far reaches of the little ship. The Cockroach cleared their place-settings and then returned to his place in the corner, watching, waiting, hoping to escape the wrath of the CO.

Under a lowering sky, they sailed across the dark depressing waters of the South China Sea, toward Cam Ranh Bay and an ammo loadout and then toward a stygian catastrophe of biblical proportions.

The Black already had orders to start firing on the west coast of IV Corps, the other side of the Mekong Delta. This time, the XO had the officers join him in the rocket loadout line, and they humped rockets for a couple of hours with the crew. A muscular sailor named Moseley hoisted the rockets off the barge and handed it to the pivot man—a muscular white boy from Louisiana named Crawly. They called him Coonass. He tried to explain to them that he was from Shreveport in northwest Louisiana and that Cajun coonasses lived in south Louisiana, but no one cared. He was and would remain Coonass.

Coonass would take the rocket, pivot a one eighty then push the sixty-pound rocket like a barbell over his head and hand it to the receiving man. The receiving man would bring it up to waist level and swing it over to the first of the linemen, who would—in a swinging motion—pass it to the next man, who would do the same until it reached the hatch, where it would go below into the bowels of the ship. It was hard, grueling work, but the officers hung in there—some better than others—until three thousand rockets were in their racks, and the Black was ready to sail for the west coast of the fetid Mekong Delta. Out of the viscous waters of the Delta, mosquitoes the size of small birds boiled, and the natives caught fish and put them on large racks to decay so that the flesh fell down between the poles that held the bones of the fish onto a baize cloth stretched below the upper level. That cloth let the juice from the decaying fish flesh strain through to the ground. The decayed flesh soon became a hot sauce that the Vietnamese loved. In the meantime, when the wind was off the land and blowing out to sea, the miasma of rotting fish drifted out toward them, and the rank cloud enveloped the Black in a rancid, putrid, malodorous haze.

At Cam Ranh, Cork made two more announcements: one, the ship would henceforth go to general quarters for nighttime firing of H&I's—harassment and interdiction—which, in the past, the night watch had handled. Second, he announced that he was modifying the ship's workday from that prescribed by Navy Regulations—from 0800 to 1630 to 0700 to 1730, with thirty minutes for lunch, a ten-hour day. If morale was already in the tank—and it was—it was now below the tank. The crew was furious, and their fury would bring repercussions for Cork one day.

The deadening heat of summer had returned, although it seemed as though it had never left. Before their first firing mission, Jack ordered the bridge crew to hoist the combat ensign. They did. Cork, from his chair, observed. The ensign broke into the air, flapping its tattered edge. "What the fuck is that rag?" Cork observed.

"That's the combat ensign, Captain," Jack said. "We always hoist it before we go into battle. It's good luck. We flew it at Hue and it brought us through it."

"I don't give a shit about what you did at Hue and I don't want that torn-up rag flying on my ship. Take the damn thing down and put up the regular ensign."

They took it down and carefully folded it and put it in a storage cabinet in the pilot house. Then they went to work.

The firing was non-stop: an airborne spotter morning and afternoon—every day—and harassment and interdiction at night. Sometimes at night a heat-seeking airplane would fly low over the jungle and find insurgents and then call-for-fire, and sometimes the Viet Cong or North Vietnamese would break in on the ship's radio frequency and string together random curse words and epithets: shit, fuck, damn, hell, ass, dick, cunt, prick. The Black's crew never knew where the cocksuckers got the words, but they laughed and fired more rockets at the radio miscreants.

After three weeks, they returned to Cam Ranh Bay and alcohol and new movies and mail. Mail. For Jack, it was a disaster that came to him in an envelope.

Amanda Brown's letter was on light blue parchment paper, and it smelled of perfume. Jack wondered if she had sprayed with her own, or slept with it next to her body, or worn it in a bra. What he read, however, shifted his focus jarringly.

Amanda was pregnant.

He wrote her back:

Jesus, Amanda. I assumed you were on the pill. Why didn't you take some precautions? I wish now I had, but we've got a problem on our hands, don't we? What do you propose to do about it?
Jack

He sent the letter, hoping that she would say that she would terminate the pregnancy. But how would she accomplish that in Japan?

That night he got drunk at the small Navy Officers' Club on the beach. A warm breeze rolled in with the waves from the South China Sea. Jack ached with what he had done and with what was going to happen to him, which he could not say with certainty but of which he had a pretty damn good idea. They listened to a small quartet with a female chanteuse, and they drank some more. Jack invited her out after the performance.

It was about 2200 when Jack stole the Navy jeep from the little Navy base, and he and the girl, Jackie, headed north toward the Air Force Base Officers' Club. Jack noticed the bunkers all along the road, and the Air Force Base was full of them. There were several piers there where civilian ships off-loaded supplies to Army Quartermasters who inventoried it and sent it in-country. Army and Air Force officers were at the club, dancing the boogaloo with nurses to 'My Girl' by the Temptations and the Four Tops doing 'Baby, I Need Your Loving' and 'Just Walk Away, Renee'. Jack danced with his 'date', and finally, too drunk to even kiss her, they headed south for the Navy's little base.

The first explosion was ahead of them. They had no idea what it was, but they knew it probably wasn't a good thing. Then there was a veritable hailstorm of rocket and mortar fire, and he and Jackie yanked the jeep off the road, and dived into a 'hooch'. The rounds were from the hills across this narrow part of the bay, and they peppered the beachfront all the way back to the Air Force Base. Jack and the nightclub singer huddled in terror. Their jeep exploded in an orange ball, and Jack knew that they were facing not only a walk back to the Navy base but a court martial about the jeep if he were caught.

The bombardment lasted for twenty long minutes and then stopped as suddenly as it had started. To the north, at the Army and Air Force bases, Jack could see a reflection of fires burning against a backdrop of ephemeral white clouds drifting silently from east to west across the sliver of a new moon. They had no jeep and no prospects of any transportation. They had only the prospect of trouble. Big trouble.

The two of them walked back to the base. The girl went into a small beach house, which had been reserved for her. Jack trudged back over the ridge and down to the Black, tied hard against the greasy steel pier. He sank into his rack and turned into the waves of dizziness that rolled toward him like surf from the Pacific on Mission Beach in San Diego. Jack would not be in the line for the rocket loadout tomorrow. He wondered what would happen with the jeep when they found the remnants of it on the road to the Army and Air Force Bases. He decided that nothing would happen; they would never find out who had stolen it, if they could even identify it. And no one saw him. Jack was clear of trouble. He smiled inwardly; then he slept.

While the sailors humped rockets, Jack got Wallis to show him how to remove and reinsert the locking pins in the launchers. "I want to know this if we ever need them again and you're gone, which you may well be."

"Well, I hope you don't ever need to do it again," Wallis said, "but here you go. It's pretty simple." Wallis had a sailor push up on the launcher barrel to take pressure off the pin. Then he took a flathead screwdriver and pushed it under the edge of the pin and then pried it out of the hole. Wallis then took pliers and pulled the pin from the launcher, letting it fall about five degrees before reinserting the pinhead. It was indeed simple, and Jack tried it and could do it, but he prayed: *no more Hue. No more Hue.*

They fired almost continuously, and general quarters for midnight firing broke their sleep for two hours, while the captain slept in his cabin. During the day the gunners mates sweated through their uniforms, and the officers through theirs. Thirst overtook them, but Cork did not have the mess decks sailors carry water to them. Dehydration invariably followed, and episodes of syncope became commonplace. Exhaustion quickly overtook the entire ship—except for Captain Cork—and between the ten-hour workday and general quarters two times a day and one time during nighttime hours, coupled with normal one-in-four watches, the men sank into debilitating fatigue. They sweated above deck, and they sweated below deck at their firing stations. The five-inch gun crew—confined to an airless gun mount—suffered gravely during their long hours at general quarters, but Cork had no mercy. He put the ship at general quarters every morning, whether firing or not, and every afternoon, also whether firing or not. Then the two hours from 2300 to 0100 came, and for those with a night watch, there was no sleep then or during the day. Cork pressed on without letup. From the XO down to the lowest seaman, the crew sank into the abyss of fatigue and despair. There would be a price to pay for their mistreatment, and it would not be long in coming. When it came, it would pack a wallop.

They received mail by 'pony express', swift boats that brought the mail to them from Cam Ranh Bay, and Amanda's letter came in early June. She told him that there was only one thing they could do: get married. And she—and her father—expected him to do the 'right thing' and marry her. The admiral would make all of the arrangements for them to marry as soon as Jack came back to Yokosuka.

He was sick. *Oh my god*, he thought. *What have I done? What am I going to do? Oh Jesus. I'm going to refuse. That's what I'm going to do. Tell 'em I'm engaged. They can send her back to the States for an abortion.*

He wrote to Amanda:

Amanda: I am not going to marry you. I am engaged to someone else. You can go back to California and get an abortion.
Jack

The debilitating heat and killing hours continued. The men sweated horribly, and from the captain, there was no mercy. Jack went to the captain's cabin. "Captain, we usually wear shorts and tee shirts down here. It would help the men a lot to change into something cooler. May I order it, sir?"

Cork sat there inscrutably, staring into nothingness. Finally, he responded: "Hell, no, XO. That must be a Bill Stockwell policy. My ship's regs prescribe the dress for the gunline. I want them in dungarees and long-sleeved denim shirts. Do you understand?"

"Yessir, but I think this is a mistake. Morale is already at rock bottom."

"Godamnit, my morale is at rock bottom, too. Keep 'em in dungarees and don't ask me again. Do you understand, XO?"

"Aye, sir." Jack left him, sitting there alone, smoking another cheap cigar.

God, he thought. *The man is crazy. He's gonna kill this crew or they're gonna kill him. I just don't understand why he is so set on changing all of Captain Stockwell's policies. For Christ's sake, Cork, give us a damn break.*

In early June, as they fired off the west coast of the Mekong Delta, a small fishing boat filled with Vietnamese men, women and children, about fifteen to twenty in all, approached the Black. As they moved closer, Cork became more apoplectic. He stood on the wing of the bridge and shouted at them to stay away, but still, they came on, closer and closer. "Put a burst of that fifty-caliber across their bow. They're as close as I'm gonna let 'em come."

Gunners Mate Third Class Wolfe fired a burst in front of the boat, whose occupants erupted in terror. But they came on, as though on automatic pilot. Cork screamed, "Goddamit I told you to stay the fuck away and I meant it.

Wolfe! Fire into that damn boat. I'll show those yellow sonsabitches why they shouldn't approach my ship."

Wolfe froze. "Goddamit, Wolfe. You heard me. Fire into that damn boat! Now!"

"Captain, I don't think that's right. Those are just civilians. I don't want to shoot them."

"Well, you damn well better do it, son, or I'm gonna court-martial you for refusing to carry out a lawful order."

"That's just it, Captain. I don't think that's lawful, ordering me to kill a bunch of innocent civilians."

"Goddamit, man, you don' know they're innocent. They may damn well be sappers, ready to put a sticky dynamite charge on our hull. Shoot the bastards."

Wolfe, frozen, did nothing.

Suddenly, Cork pushed him aside and grabbed the gun. Then he fired.

Jack had never seen what a fifty-caliber machine-gun could do to human flesh, only to the vegetation along the Perfume River, where the gun had chewed it up like lettuce, but he saw it now.

The slugs hit flesh with a loud 'thunk', then the flesh exploded. Bodies flew in and off the boat. Screams punctuated the staccato bursts from the machine-gun. Cork continued firing. And then it was over. Bodies littered the water around the boat. A few remained in the boat. All were dead, and the water around the boat was red with blood, which also pooled in the bottom of the boat.

"I told you idiots that I was gonna show you how to kill Commies for Christ and now I have. Remember it, you puke. Wolfe, you fuckin' coward, are gonna be court-martialed."

True to his word, Cork convened a special court martial, which heard the case. Paul Sessums represented Wolfe. The court exonerated him, and Cork called the three of them, Henderson, Duvall and Burwell into his cabin and cursed and threatened them. Badly. He concluded with, "You fuckin' pukes are gonna be sorry for this. I guaran-damn-tee you. Just wait. I'll get my chance and you can by god bet that I won't let it slip by. Stand fuckin' by, you teatheads."

Cork convened the wardroom on nights when there was no firing to play poker in the wardroom. With one on watch, there were six of them. They played quarter ante and a dollar limit. Jack had grown up in Concord—a poker town—playing with good players, and he knew how to play poker.

They had been playing for a little over an hour when Jack hit a full house, three kings over two threes. At the end of the hand, only Cork and Jack remained in the game. The others had all folded, and they watched the spectacle unfold with unease twisting their faces. Finally, all bets were in, and the captain laid down his hand. "Too bad, XO. I got an ace high flush." He smiled smugly and reached for the pot.

The XO wavered. He knew that he ought to throw his in and concede. But he couldn't. So, he did it: "Captain, I've got a full house." And then he laid down his cards.

Cork stared at them for a long fifteen seconds or so. Jack took a deep breath. The others looked on in horror, in terror. Suddenly, Cork screamed: "Goddamit you sonofabitchin' bastard asshole mother fucking cunt pissant shithead." With that, he scraped up part of the pot and threw it at Jack. Then he grabbed the cards remaining in the deck and threw them at Jack, also. Then, with his cigar in his mouth he stormed out of the wardroom, slamming the door, and went up the ladder to his cabin where he slammed his door so hard they could feel it in the wardroom.

"Jesus," Jack said. "I won't play with him again."

The others just sat there, stunned at what they had just seen.

"God, XO," Liam McNamara said, "that is conduct unbecoming an officer if I ever saw it. You ought to report it to the Commodore."

"Liam, I may do a lot of things but that is not one of them. I'll bury that in my memory and in the graveyard of officer sins." Jack shook his head sadly. "Jesus," he said. Just Jesus.

On June 23, after repeated problems with the port engine, they received orders to return to Yokosuka for a major overhaul. First there would be the requisite stop in Hong Kong—Cork was an east coast man and had never been there—so they pulled into their little pier, and the ship's company, after two hard months on the gunline, firing non-stop, went ashore and ran wild.

A sailor named Francis went crazy in a bar and beat up a Chinese whore. The British authorities arrested him. A British military policeman showed up at the Black and informed them of the arrest. "I would go on and get him out this afternoon. You don't want him staying overnight. There is no telling what will happen to him."

Jack was ashore, so Ensign Henderson, one of the two duty officers, went to the captain and told him that he was going to get him out.

"The hell you say. He's spending the night. Teach him a goddam lesson."

"Captain, the Brit says get him out, that bad shit happens in there overnight."

"Well, let it happen. I don't give a shit. Go get him tomorrow morning."

Three Chinese men came to Francis at about 0200. They stripped him, and each took a turn raping him anally. He bled. And bled. And bled.

When he returned to the ship, the word had already swept through ship's company like a bad smell. They told Francis what Cork had done.

He would not forget.

Jack caught the USS Waddell, which was headed for Yokosuka at 25 knots. He took with him a list of items that needed repair on the Black, and he was to meet with the yard foreman assigned to the Black, so he could line up the necessary work crews to get started upon the Black's arrival. But there was one more thing he had to deal with: Amanda was by now about three months pregnant and maybe showing, and there were Admiral and Mrs. Brown also with whom to deal. His stomach churned when he thought of it, because he feared what the outcome of those dealings would be.

The Waddell was a definite step or two or five up from the Black. Its wardroom was plush and spacious, and its officers welcoming and curious about the Black, of which they had heard from their own time on the Vietnam gunline. They asked him how rapidly the Black could fire, about the explosive fire of the rockets, how the Black rode in heavy seas, and Jack regaled them with sea stories of heavy seas, firing and being fired upon at Rach Gia and Hue, her speed—twelve knots top—and taking their meals out of the enlisted men's mess.

Jack was especially interested in the navigator, Bill Barrett, because Barrett did not do the navigating himself. He allowed his chief and petty officers to navigate, and he just oversaw their operation. In the wardroom, Jack sat with him.

"Where are you from, Jack? You've got a helluva accent," Bill asked him.

"Mississippi, Bill. How about you?"

"Davenport, Iowa. Did you go to OCS or do ROTC?"

"I went to OCS. Entered the day Kennedy was assassinated. How about you?"

"ROTC at the University of Iowa. I hear OCS was tough."

"Tough enough. They said it was the academic equivalent of twenty-three semester hours in college. That wasn't what was so tough about it, though. It was the lack of sleep that got me. Up at five-thirty and hit the rack at ten-thirty. That's a seventeen-hour day and if you had the evening, mid or morning watches, you got even less. The worst thing was what they called roving patrol. I had it twice, both times in the middle of the night. All I did was walk around a defined area looking for people trying to break in to one of the buildings, like there were Communist spies trying to steal our secrets. Every hour I had to check in with the officer of the watch. If I had an alarm clock, I would have slept in between but I didn't. Both times it was cold. In the twenties with that bad Newport wind. I almost died."

"I had heard about OCS but never about that aspect of it. Jeez, I'm glad I missed that. Do you play cards on the Black River?"

"Yeah, we play poker and gin."

"Want to play some gin with me?"

"Absolutely."

He was the best gin player Jack had ever seen. Barrett cut Jack to pieces. "God almighty, Bill. I've never seen anyone like you. Do you ever lose?"

"Yeah. Sometimes. But I'm getting good cards tonight for some reason. Try me again tomorrow night."

"They watched a movie—'Rosemary's Baby'—together, and then Jack went up to the bridge with Bill for the evening—2000 to 2400—watch. They, with the captain's permission, let Jack take the conn, and he made two turns. Jesus, she handles beautifully. What a change from the Black, which is so top heavy that you never know what the wind is going to do to you and where you are going to be when you come out of a turn."

The Boatswains Mate of the watch brought them hot coffee, and they drank it and smoked cigarettes, whose cones glowed in the darkness of the bridge. Outside, there was a three-quarters moon, and Jack took the sextant and shot and plotted a moon line to see if he could make it work. He returned from the pilot house to the bridge.

"How'd it go, Jack?" Bill asked.

"Like shit. I've never had any luck with those damn things."

"Nor have I. No luck with moon lines and no luck with sun lines. Waste of time."

"Do you stay in the BOQ when you are in port, Bill?"

"No, I'm married. We live out on the economy. How about you?"

"I'm single. Our officer's quarters on the Black are so shitty that they let us stay in the BOQ. We do the usual stuff: go to the JO dances at the O Club, go out on the economy and pick up Japanese bar girls, play golf when the weather's warm and flag football when it's cooler."

"Doesn't sound bad. We have a couple of children so that's what I do when I'm in port. We do have a sitter so we go to the O Club for movie night and roast beef night on Fridays. The problem I have is we spend so much time on the line. It's usually three or four months down and one back. How about you?"

"Yeah, that's about right. We go to Subic about halfway through our gunline-time and Hong Kong on the way back. There's always a lot of repair work that we need in Yoko so that keeps us busy overseeing the yard people."

"Well, maybe you can come to the O Club with us for movie night. There are a lot of round-eyed nurses at the hospital in Yoko. Grab one and come on with us."

"Sounds great. Will do."

They stopped in Okinawa to take on fuel and water, and Jack and Bill visited the Air Force Officers' Club together with four other officers from the Waddell. It was a happy time for Jack: no responsibilities, no Cork, no navigation, no sweat. They sat in the darkly paneled club and drank and smoked and told war stories. None of theirs could match Jack's, and the Waddell officers were amazed at the hostile fire they had taken and the disasters that had threatened them. He told them of Cork and the Tokyo expressway, of Cohen and the clap, of the JO bunkroom and its omnipresent smell. They laughed and loved it.

The message came two days' out from Yokosuka. It was from Comphibron Eleven: "Have Lt. Houston report to Comphibron Eleven upon arrival." *Ship's repair business,* Jack thought. *But I wonder why they are getting involved. That's shipyard stuff and they don't usually get in the middle of that.*

The Waddell pulled into Yokosuka on June 28. Now, he was back with an enormous cloud named Amanda Brown hanging over him like grim death. He hoped that his letter had been sufficient and that she had left by now. He hoped, but he knew that hope in a situation like that was thin, watery soup.

Yokosuka

Among the crowd of women on the pier there were two women whom Jack knew. They were the two married women from the Officers' Club, one with whom he had slept back in March. They looked at him, up on the wing of the bridge, and he could see doom descend on them like a shroud. It was enveloping him, too, for he didn't know which one of the officers belonged to his fuck-mate. Soon, the officers' brow went down, and he watched as the Waddell's officers exited the ship to waiting wives and nurse girlfriends. And then it happened. Bill Barrett went to Jack's bedmate, and they embraced and Jack's stomach turned. *Oh god,* he thought. *Oh god. Not Bill. Jesus. Not him. I will never do that again. Never again with a married woman. I swear to god I won't.* He waited until they had left the pier before he went down.

The next day, he reported to the Comphibron Eleven staff. The Commodore called him in. "Jack," he said, "I've a message from Admiral Brown. He wants to see you ASAP at his headquarters. He had sent a message to your ship and they sent it to me. You need to get on up there right away."

"Aye, sir. Will do."

"Do you have any idea what this is about?"

"Yessir, I know exactly what it's about."

"Well…what?"

"Nothing that concerns the ship or you or your staff, sir. That's all I want to say about it."

"Very well. Get moving."

Jack drove his MGB up the mountain to the base commander's headquarters. He checked in with the admiral's adjutant, who smiled smugly at him. Finally, Admiral Brown buzzed for him to enter.

"Hello, Jack. Close the door and have a seat."

After he was seated, Admiral Brown cleared his throat, lit a Winston, and put his feet up on his desk. "How was your trip back, Jack? I bet the Waddell was a nicer ride than you are accustomed to."

"Yessir, it was a nice change."

"Well, you know why I wanted you here. We've got a situation on our hands and we need to resolve it. Don't we?"

"Yessir. Are you aware of what I wrote to Amanda?"

"Yes, I am. And I'm sorry about your engagement. But the truth is, we're Catholic and there's not going to be any trip back to the States for an abortion. You're going to marry Amanda and that's it."

Jack's stomach churned. Weakness flowed from his head down his trunk into his legs. "Sir, I don't think that's fair."

"It's fair. You got Amanda pregnant and now you've got to make it right. The marriage will take place in Tokyo tomorrow. I've made all of the arrangements for it so make your peace with it and let's get it done. Okay?"

Jack said nothing.

"Okay, Jack?" He asked it with emphasis this time.

"I don't know what to do, Admiral. I'm engaged to a girl back in the States and she's coming out here next month to marry me. I just can't say no, don't come."

"You can and you will. You are marrying Amanda and that's it. You write your girl and tell her not to come, that you're marrying someone else."

"Admiral, with all due respect, I don't believe that's a lawful order and I don't think I have to comply with it and marry Amanda and I'm not going to do it. I'm in love with someone else who is coming out here to marry me and I'm going to marry her."

"Well, Jack, I had hoped it wouldn't come to this. I had hoped you would do the right thing and step up to the plate like a man and do what you should do but apparently, you're not so you have forced my hand and I'm going to play the trump card."

"And what is that, sir?"

"You may remember a little jeep incident in Cam Ranh Bay, right?"

Jack froze. He swallowed hard.

"Cat got your tongue, Jack? All of a sudden, you've gone quiet on me."

The admiral looked at Jack and smiled.

"Well, here's the deal. You stole and destroyed government property and then didn't report it. Both of those offenses are court martial offenses and I have here sitting on my desk papers requesting a general court martial for you. A general court martial would likely put you in Leavenworth for a couple of years and result in a dishonorable discharge. I have sat on these papers for the better part of a month now but I'm ready to move forward and order the court martial if you don't do what's right. If you do the right thing, I'll lose these papers and that'll be that."

Jack's face drained of color, and his throat tightened. *Jesus,* he thought, *how in the fuck did they pin it on me? Who knew? How?*

"Jack, it's a pretty airtight case. They have a witness who has given a statement that she was with you when it happened. She will testify that you stole the jeep and took her to the Army and Air Force bases at Cam Ranh Bay and that there was a mortar attack as you returned that destroyed the stolen jeep. There is another witness—a sailor who was on watch—who saw you two take the jeep. He didn't know you but he knew her and that's what led them to interview her the next day before she left for Saigon. I've got her name here and his, as well, and I can read you their statements if you like."

"No sir, that won't be necessary. I guess that leaves me with no choice but to marry Amanda."

"Jack, I'm sorry it came to this but you left me no choice. Now this is going to be a quick, quiet affair. I've had my legal officer check out the requirements and it's pretty simple. You'll go to Tokyo tomorrow with Amanda and fill out the papers there and they'll declare you married and that'll be it. There's not much to it. I'll get you quarters on the base and we've got furniture to furnish it and you and Amanda can move in—it'll take a week or so to get all of that done—and wait on the baby. You can stay at the BOQ until your quarters are ready. Okay?"

"I guess so, Admiral. I mean, what else can I do? What choice do I have?"

"You know the answer to that as well as I do, Jack. None. So, let's get on with it. My driver will take you and Amanda to Tokyo tomorrow. You'll need two witnesses so I'm sending Byron and Carolyn King with you. Amanda is not an early riser and she's having some morning sickness so it will be an afternoon trip. Driver will pick you up at the BOQ at 1300. Okay?"

Jack smiled laconically. "Yessir," he said sadly. "Am I free to go?"

"Oh, don't act that way. Of course you're free to go. You're not under arrest. Go on and write your girlfriend back in the States and get that over with and let's get on with the wedding tomorrow. My driver will get you at 1300 at the BOQ. Be ready."

Jack walked out of the admiral's headquarters into the heat of summer, and he stood for a moment and looked out over the base sprawling before him. *Goddamn,* he thought. *Goddamn.*

Amanda was cheerful, almost jaunty when they picked him up the next day. Inwardly, Jack groaned. But what could he do? She and her admiral father had him by the short hairs. He could do nothing but write to Melanie and tell her not to come.

That night at the admiral's quarters they made him call his mother and tell her that he had married Amanda in a civil service in Tokyo that day. His mother, stunned, wanted details. *Who is this girl? How old is she? How did you meet her? When did you meet her? Why so suddenly? Why have you waited until now to tell me?* He bobbed and weaved and finessed the last question and told her that it was done. There would be no marriage ceremony, just the civil service in the Japanese magistrate's court that they had done that afternoon. His mother wept softly on the other end. "I'm out of time, Mama. Bye." And he hung up.

The Black returned to Yokosuka, and Jack announced to Cork and the wardroom that he and Amanda Brown were married. There was stunned silence. Then Liam McNamara spoke: "XO, this is a surprise. That's all. I didn't even know you were dating her. But it's wonderful. We'll have a big celebration. An admiral's daughter. Man, that's top-drawer."

"Thanks, Liam." The others formed a line and dutifully congratulated him, but skepticism floated in the smoky haze that overhung the wardroom. Through the heavy miasma of Cork's rancid cigar smoke, they smelled a rat, and the rat was Jack.

He and Amanda moved into a small house on base five days later. There was a waiting list for base housing comprised of officers far senior to Jack, but it was the admiral's golden rule: he who has the gold makes the rule. And the admiral had the gold, and he made the rule, and there was not a thing anyone could do about it except grouse.

The Letter to Melanie

It was the most difficult thing he had ever done, but he did what he had to do and wrote to her:

Dear Melanie:
    This is the hardest letter I have ever had to write—and probably the hardest thing I have ever had to do—and I begin it by saying forgive me. I have screwed up terribly and gotten a woman pregnant out here and must marry her. I do not love her. It was a one-night deal, and I shouldn't have done it, but I

was drunk, and I did. I don't intend to stay married long and will get a divorce as soon as I can and come to you, whom I love more than anything in the world. I can't ask you to wait for me, but if you are still unattached when I get out of this marriage that I am being forced into, I will come find you. I am so sorry and hope you can forgive me.

With all my love,
Jack

Jack did not expect to hear from Melanie, but she wrote, and he received the letter with surprise and pain when he saw the familiar handwriting. His stomach churned as he opened the light blue envelope.

Dear Jack:
Needless to say, I was stunned to receive your letter. Frankly, I didn't—and don't—know what to say, thus the delay in answering you. What I feel is a horrible sense of betrayal. I had, once again, put all of my apples into your basket, and like my trip last Christmas to San Francisco, except far worse, you pulled the rug on me. It was so bad that after I read your letter I had to go to bed. I will never forgive you for this, and that is all I am going to say.
Good luck with your 'marriage', I hope you enjoy it.

Melanie

God, it's like a hundred-pound weight has fallen on me. I don't think I can get up and get out of this chair. I feel like shooting myself, like suicide is the only way out of this mess. I've lost the girl I love more than anything in the world, and I've likely lost her forever. Oh, god, what have I done? I've thrown away my whole damn life.

Aching, Jack felt like he was in a soulless netherworld, and he felt almost repulsed by Amanda Brown. But they were married, and there was no way out of it for Jack, and so inwardly, he wept. And nights he drank himself to sleep, with three or so drinks before dinner and three or four after. He was haunted by the knowledge that Melanie, beautiful Melanie, was gone forever and that he had blown that relationship to smithereens, as though it had been hit by a sixteen-inch shell off the USS New Jersey.

Life with Amanda in their base housing settled into a soul-numbing routine: Jack and Amanda spent most nights either at the Officers Club for drinks—many drinks—or at the admiral's quarters, where drinks were also plentiful. Amanda couldn't even make coffee, so they ate at home only what Jack could cook on the grill: steaks and hamburgers and chicken. Hung-over, he drove each morning to the Black. The quality of his work declined precipitously, but Cork, fearing the wrath of Admiral Brown, said nothing. Jack, through his base commander father-in-law, had Cork by the gonads. Jack no longer made inspections of messing and berthing spaces, and the ship sank into a filthy abyss, while Jack sat in his stateroom, hung-over each day, brooding and drinking coffee and smoking and aching for Melanie and for all that he had lost.

Strangely, Amanda did not look pregnant. She looked like she had gained some weight, but there was little stomach and no morning sickness. Jack asked her about it, but she told him that it varied from woman to woman and that she had a large frame and could handle it. She would, she said, begin showing at five or six months. Jack accepted her explanation and soldiered on with a woman he didn't love.

Amanda had a second car that her father had given her when she came to Japan, so she slept late and then went to the Officers' Club for winey lunches and bridge with the wives of her father's staff. They learned Japanese flower arranging, learned origami, and went to exercise classes in the club gym. Each week they would devote one afternoon to shopping on the economy. She bought two Japanese chests—tonsus—and a mahogany hibachi: a cooking chest with a copper basin for the coals and a myriad of oriental vases, wood carvings and Japanese prints. In Tokyo, she bought jewelry, and a stereo and a Nikon camera for Jack, who was stunned by the amount of money she spent. He said nothing. He just drank.

Late in the afternoon, she would return to the house, set up the bar, and get ready to have people in for drinks, or go out for drinks or dress for the Officers' Club. And each day in that cycle brought Jack closer to the black dog that awakened him every morning around three and told him all that he had lost and how he was trapped in a black hole that was getting deeper by the day.

Underway Training

The Navy, like any large bureaucracy, has boxes that it likes to check, and underway refresher training is such a box. The Black River, although it had been in combat operations for most of the last two years, was selected by its staff for this honor, and so in mid-July, the Black's staff came aboard, and the Black, without any preparation, got underway down Tokyo Bay to a designated U. S. Navy training area that was off-limits to shipping. But two days before she left the pier, the senior enlisted men met. And planned. Their revenge for Cork's maltreatment of the crew was at hand.

Jack navigated and, hung-over, still did it like clockwork. Cork was his usual self in the heavy traffic of the Bay, storming from side to side, shouting confusing and often conflicting orders, and generally sowing mayhem on the Black's bridge.

"Goddam it, Mr. McNamara, wake the fuck up. I want you to maneuver to avoid these fuckin' freighters."

"Sir, Mr. Sessums and the XO are recommending course and speed in accordance with the international rules of the road and the XO's chart calculations. Do you want me to disregard those recommendations?"

"I want you to keep us out of a collision, Mr. McNamara. That's what I want. Now do you think you can do that?"

"Sir, I think I can if you let me follow Mr. Sessums's recommendations off the maneuvering board and based on the rules of the road, when we are either burdened to maintain course and speed or privileged to maneuver. If I can't do that, the other ships won't know what we are doing. *Sir!*" He said the last word with emphasis. Cork's head snapped. He knew an insult when he heard one, and that 'sir' was definitely one.

"I heard that, Mr. McNamara. And I won't forget it either. Yes, I want you to listen to my orders and relay them to the pilot house. You got it?"

"Yessir, I do. But I want you to take the conn, sir. I don't want my name in the log as having the conn if you're giving the orders."

"Very well. Tell the pilot house that the captain has the conn and standby to relay orders."

"Aye, Sir." Then he spoke into the voice tube to the pilot house: "This is Mr. McNamara. The captain has the conn."

From the pilot house, "Aye, Sir. The captain has the conn."

Then came a bewildering jumble of orders. "XO, give me a course!"

"Sir, I recommend that you maintain course and speed."

"I don't give a good goddam what you recommend."

"But sir, you asked me for a course recommendation and I gave it to you. Do you not want any other course recommendations?"

"Yes…no, I got bogies all over the place. You," he said to the frightened sound-powered phone operator, "ask Mr. Sessums what that contact out there at one-three-five is doing?"

The messenger, an insipid little monkey named Halbert, spoke into the sound-powered phone. Then: "Captain, Mr. Sessums says he recommends that you maintain course and speed. The contact at one-three-five is going to pass well astern of us."

"Goddam that fuckin' teathead. I'll show you bastards how to drive a ship. Right full rudders! Come right to course two-three-five."

Jack plotted his course on the chart. "Sir, that course is going to run us aground in about eight minutes. I recommend coming left to one-seven-zero."

"Fuck!" the captain shouted. "Goddamit, doesn't anyone around here know anything? Jesus. Come left to one-seven-zero."

The staff observer's eyes were as big as a shark's, but instead of savagery, they reflected fear and bewilderment. He walked over to Jack's wing of the bridge. "Good god! Is he always like this?"

"Always," Jack said quietly. "And this is really nothing. He's just warming up."

Set and drift calculations determine what course is necessary to put the ship back on course after currents push her off course. The navigator is supposed to determine how much the current has pushed the ship off the course and where it will be in three minutes, then crank in a course recommendation that will take the ship that far above the course to restore her to the recommended course in three minutes.

Jack had always done those in his head because it was faster and just as accurate. He did so now and made his recommendation. "Sir I recommend that you come right to one-seven-three."

"Very well, XO. Helmsman, come right to course one-seven-three."

The staff officer, Lieutenant Commander Sistrunk spoke: "XO, that is not the way you're supposed to do set and drift calculations. You didn't do it on the chart. You should have drawn the triangle above the recommended course to determine the new course that you recommended. I am going to gig you for that."

"What'd you say Mr. Sistrunk?" the captain screamed, his voice a couple of octaves higher than normal.

"I said I was going to gig the navigator for not doing his set and drift calculation correctly. And I'm going to gig you, Captain Cork, for not following recommendations from CIC for maneuvers to avoid and for not following the XO's course recommendations. That's three major gigs and we've barely gotten out of port."

The captain sat heavily down. "You're what?" he bellowed.

"I think you heard me, Captain."

"Goddam you, you fuckin' staff puke. I am going to have your ass. You just wait. I'm keelhauling you to the Commodore. You just wait and see how you like that, goddamnit."

"That's your privilege, Captain."

"And XO, goddam you, do the fuckin' calculations right. I don't see how you can blow something so basic as set and drift. And that'll go in your fitness report."

"Aye, sir," Jack said. "That will go in my fitness report."

Cork's head snapped at the XO. "Are you being a smartass, XO?"

"No sir, Captain. I was just repeating what you said for the quartermaster's log. And the truth is, I can do set and drift calculations in my head that are just as accurate as those I do on the chart and a helluva lot faster."

Riggio was busy writing the CO-XO colloquy into the navigator's log.

"Strike that, Riggio. I don't want that in the log. That's between the XO and me. You understand, son?"

"Aye, sir. Strike that'll go in your fuckin' fitness report and all between you and the XO that followed it."

"Goddamit, is everybody up here being a smart ass. Goddamit, I'm goin' below before I say or do something' I shouldn't. Take the conn, Mr. McNamara."

"Aye Sir. Boats, this is Mr. McNamara. I have the deck and the conn."

"Aye, Sir. Mr. McNamara has the deck and the conn."

Cork stormed off the bridge. "My god," Lieutenant Commander Sistrunk groaned. "I've never seen anything like that. I'm going to have to write him up in a report that the rest of the staff is not going to believe."

And so it went. Cork stayed in his stateroom until the XO reported to him that they were the training area, and then Cork returned to the bridge. Their first exercise was to fire the five-inch gun.

Jack went to CIC, Paul Sessums went to the bridge as OOD, and Liam McNamara took over the bridge gunnery operations. As they cruised slowly along, a plane appeared pulling an airborne drone. "Bandit at two-eight-five," Fincher reported from CIC to the bridge. "Course one eight zero, range thirty-six hundred and fifty yards."

Wallis cranked the data into the gunfire control mechanism, and the five-inch gun rotated to starboard. Then came the report from the gun mount: "Locked on and tracking, Sir."

Liam McNamara: "Very well, Mr. Henderson. Standby."

Cork's various transgressions against the crew were just about ready to come home. McNamara turned to the captain. "Sir, gun mount reports locked on and tracking. The line-of-sight is clear. Request permission to commence firing."

"Very well," Cork said. "Commence firing."

"Commence firing, Mr. Henderson!"

No one on the ship expected what happened next. The proximity fuse exploded just after it came out of the barrel, about two-hundred yards off the ship's starboard-side. The explosion rocked the Black, and the percussion rolled across the bridge like a tidal wave.

"Jesus god, Mr. McNamara. What the fuck?" Cork screamed.

"Sir, something's wrong with the proximity fuse. I don't know what. Let me try to find out."

By now, Cork was a screaming madman. Shrill curses exploded on the bridge like the prematurely exploding shell. Then came the clincher. "Mr. Henderson doesn't know, Captain. He wants to try again."

"Goddamit, Mr. Sistrunk, order the drone plane back. We'll pick him up on his reciprocal course this time and do it right."

Once again, Fincher reported course, speed and distance, and Wallis cranked the data into the fire control mechanism. The gun mount adjusted. And once again, the shell exploded just after it left the ship, but this time at only a hundred yards off the ship.

Cork screamed: "Goddamit McNamara. You and Henderson are responsible for this. And you're gonna pay. You understand me?"

"Aye, sir," Liam McNamara said. "Mr. Henderson and I are responsible for this and we are going to pay."

Cork turned to Sistrunk. "Have you ever seen us fire the rockets, Mr. Sistrunk?"

"No, I haven't, Captain, and I'd like to."

"Well, let me show you. My crew is really good at that. Standby."

"Mr. McNamara, prepare to fire rockets. Port side launchers."

"Aye, aye, sir. Port side launchers."

McNamara sent word to CIC and his men below to standby to fire all four of the port side rocket launchers. In CIC, Wallis and Jack made necessary preparations. Jack reported ready to the bridge.

"All right, Mr. McNamara, go to it."

McNamara informed the XO. On the bridge, the captain and Mr. Sistrunk moved to the port side to watch the pyrotechnics display, a smug smile of satisfaction on the captain's face. *This would do it,* he thought. *This will make it all right again. Sistrunk's never seen anything like this. It'll blow him away.*

The XO gave the command for the port side launchers to fire one round each, simultaneously.

There was a loud swish as the rockets roared out of the *starboard-side* launchers, then a loud scream.

"Goodgodamighty!" Cork screamed in a voice rife with harrow. "What the goddam hell is goin' on, Mr. McNamara?"

Liam McNamara said that he didn't know. Cork and Sistrunk wheeled around, Cork's face twisted with rage. "What the fuck?" Cork screamed in a falsetto, his throat tightening like his jaw. "Oh god, no. Not this. Not the rockets. Nooooo."

"Jesus," McNamara said.

The speaker box in CIC roared. All Jack could hear was a cacophony of curses: shit, cunt, fuck, goddam, bastards. Then, "XO, get your ass up here! On the double!"

"Crowley, hurry up and ask the bridge what happened."

He did. "Sir, we fired from the starboard-side instead of the port side. Captain and the observer were on the port side. Captain Cork's having a fit."

"Oh, shit," Jack said.

He reported to the bridge.

Cork was apoplectic. "What in the fuck is goin' on here? Goddamit, XO, you can't even fire the right launchers. I'm puttin' the whole damn ship in hack tonight and you're gonna get this shit worked out or I'm going to start the court martials on all of you. Secure from general quarters. Mr. Sistrunk, we're taking her back in."

Mr. Sistrunk was too busy making notes to reply. Jack took over navigation. They started home.

True to his word, Cork slapped the entire ship in hack—'corkscrewed' them—and told the XO to get his ass in gear and get this damn mess straightened out by tomorrow. Then he went home.

Jack called a meeting of the officers in the wardroom. "Look guys, we're in deep shit and we got to work our way out or we'll probably not see the light of day for the rest of the time we're in Yokosuka. Liam and Hinky, any idea what happened with the five-inch gun fuses today?"

"Someone set them that way, XO," Liam said. "That's the only explanation. Someone sabotaged the fuses. And I bet you if he keeps slapping us with hack there is going to be more of this stuff."

"Okay, Hinky. I want you to check the five-inch proximity fuses before we fire tomorrow. Okay?"

"Yessir, XO. Will do."

"Next, Liam, how the hell did we fire from the wrong side?"

"XO, I don't know. The men say that they just heard wrong."

"Well, that's a crock. I clearly told the port side launchers to fire. You think it was intentional?"

"Probably, XO," McNamara said. "They hate Captain Bluto Corkscrew."

"Well, tell him they're hurting everyone on this ship in trying to get to the CO. Tell them that they will not see any more liberty if they keep this shit up. Okay, Liam?"

"Yes sir. But, XO, do you agree with all of this crap the captain's doing?"

"It doesn't matter whether I agree or not. He's the CO and I'm the XO and my job is to carry out his orders and see that you carry out his orders. It's not for you and me to second-guess him. We're just going to do our duty. Okay?"

"Okay, XO." McNamara looked at the XO skeptically, a quizzical look on his face. *How the hell can he enforce these orders? How can he not admit that Cork's crazy? I know he thinks it. God, I couldn't do it if I were the XO.*

"Mr. Sessums, are you ready to go in communications? They'll be working on you tomorrow."

"We're ready, XO. I think we'll be fine."

"And engineering, Mr. Tyson. How do you stand?"

"We're in good shape, XO. Should be fine. Morale really sucks, though, and all of this hack is killing us."

"I can understand that but it's not a damn thing we can do about that. Tell the crew that the way to get out of hack is to do well in the rest of refresher training."

The officers said they would. Then Delos Reyes served them dinner: beef tips over noodles, English peas and fruit cobbler with ice cream. They watched a movie, and for the first time in weeks, Jack did not drink himself to sleep.

They got underway the next day and headed down the Tokyo freeway. It was a reprise of the day before, with Cork running about the bridge shouting commands while Mr. Sistrunk gigged him right and left. Jack performed perfectly and took them—in spite of Cork's dysfunctional turns—to the firing range, performing set and drift calculations on the chart in the prescribed manner. They went to general quarters and awaited the drone. It appeared, traveling fore to aft down the Black's starboard-side. CIC picked it up on radar and gave readings to Wallis, who cranked in the numbers to the fire control system, and then the mount reported 'locked on and tracking' and cut loose.

The first round almost hit the plane, which was 150 yards in front of the drone. Cork stood in stunned silence. Then he exploded. "Goddamit to hell Mr. McNamara I'm gonna court-martial your sorry ass for incompetence and the whole damn gunnery crew, from CIC to the last man in the mount."

The five-inch fun continued spitting rounds everywhere but at the drone. Cork screamed 'stop firing', but they continued hurling rounds wildly into the air. Then, after Liam McNamara got them stopped the engines stopped, and the Black went dead in the water.

"What the fuck's goin' on?" Cork sputtered his eyes as big as saucers. "Get Mr. Tyson on the phone."

The Zit came online. "What the hell's the matter down there, Tyson? We're dead in the fuckin' water."

"Captain, someone put water in one of the tanks. We're switching over to the other one now."

Cork slammed down the phone. He looked skyward and wailed. "Why is this happening' to me? My god, what have I done to deserve this? Mr. Sessums, call the plane and have them return to base. We're done shooting for today."

Sessums picked up the radio handset and called the plane. There was nothing. The radio was down. Not working. On the fritz. Dead. Lieutenant Commander Sistrunk was scribbling on his steno pad as fast as he could.

Cork sunk into his chair. His head slumped almost into his lap. He shook it morosely. Slowly. Sadly. "Okay, Mr. Sessums, secure from general quarters. Take her home as soon as we get power."

"Aye, Sir."

One of the engines came back online, and at five knots, they started for Yokosuka. The gyro compasses failed, the radar went down, they were unable to fix their position, and they were forced to travel back by visual sightings of known objects. Jack went topside and took her home.

"Goddamit! I can't trust any of you assholes to take her in. I'll do it myself."

Cork took the conn and began giving orders from the wing of the bridge. Liam McNamara relayed them to the pilot house over the voice tube, and the lee helmsman sent the speed orders to engineering by the engine order telegraph. As Cork approached the pier at a forty-five-degree angle, he ordered the engines back one-third. Liam McNamara relayed the command to the pilot house. The boatswain's mate of the watch acknowledged the command. The lee helmsman rang it up for engineering.

Nothing happened.

"All engines back two-thirds," Cork shouted. Nothing happened.

"Jesus god," the captain screamed. "All back full emergency."

Liam McNamara shouted the command into the voice tube again. There was nothing but the sound of the Black's bow crashing into the pier. Wood splinters flew. The line-handling crew on the pier scattered like the line handlers at Cam Rahn Bay. The Black plowed ahead. Cork ran from side to side, screaming expletives and epithets. Finally, a few feet into the pier, the Black stopped. Cork had violated one of the fundamental unwritten rules of the fleet: Never piss off your entire crew. Eventually, they will find a way to get back at you. And the Black's crew had.

Mr. Sistrunk shook his head sadly. He left. Cork said that he was going to court-martial, "every damn fuckin' one of those engineers." With the entire crew in hack, he stormed off the ship. Liam McNamara estimated that they would have upward of thirty court martials in the next few weeks.

The next day, the Commodore summoned Cork to headquarters and in front of the senior staff officers, chewed him from stem to stern. Brunini went over Sistrunk's report, as well as those of the other observers. "You *flunked* underway training, Cork. *Flunked it!* How in god's name do you *flunk* underway training? I've had ships that did not do well in it. And I've had ships that excelled in it. But I have never by god had a ship, or even heard of a ship, *flunking* underway training. Captain Cork, you have set a new record for incompetence and by god, I won't forget this."

"Now get your ass out of here and get your ship squared away. I have orders for you to go to Tacloban in the Philippines down on Leyte for the Leyte Gulf festival in October. The Black River was Seventh Fleet ship of the year under your predecessor so you have the honor of representing our country to celebrate MacArthur's invasion there and the victory over the Japanese fleet in the naval battles of Leyte Gulf. The festival is twenty and twenty-one October. You will be on the line till then and we'll schedule you to go to Subic and get ready and then go on down to Leyte. You better not screw this up or I will send your ass back to the States. Get to it."

Cork returned to the ship that afternoon and announced that he was staying overnight and that "by God I'm going to get this ship squared damn away." His first order was that the entire ship was in hack. Again. Then he issued a myriad of confusing and oftentimes conflicting orders with respect to what the officers and crew were to do to rectify 'this goddam mess'. He wanted the ship cleaned from bow to stern. He wanted the men to perform concomitant drills at general quarters. He wanted the entire ship's company to eat 'C' rations for supper. He ordered them to wear dress blues to perform maintenance in the engineering spaces, in the bilges and on all of the weapons, all filthy tasks at best.

The crew was up all night performing various drills and in between drills, cleaning the ship. Cork sat on the bridge, timing everything they did, especially the time it took them to go to general quarters and to get the hatches closed and secured. Whatever they did was insufficient, so they did it over and over and over. Finally, Cork retired to his stateroom and the men to their racks.

Cork had a brand-new maroon Mercury cougar with a black, fabric-covered top. He had bought it just before coming to Japan, and it was his pride and joy. The next morning, after breakfast and before chewing anyone's ass, he walked out onto the quarterdeck to ensure that it was squared away in accordance with the barrage of orders he had issued the day before. One of the orders was that an officer would stand each of the four-hour day watches in dress blues, with a sword at his side and medals on his chest. That was a new requirement. Officers had never stood quarterdeck watches in port. Previously, each officer served as a command duty officer for the day. Only enlisted men stood quarterdeck watches.

T. P. Burwell had the quarterdeck. Although he didn't know it, his moment under Cork's heavy hand had come.

Cork studied every detail of the quarterdeck: the brass, to ensure it had been polished. The fancy-work—small white ropes woven and wound together and draping from the white tarp that covered the quarterdeck. He wanted it so clean that it 'sparkled'.

Then Cork looked out at his car. He screamed in horror and rage, threw his head back and wailed to the sky: "Godammit! Nooooo. Not this. Oh Jesus, not this." Then came a gallimaufry of curses, orders, and epithets: 'shit, fuck, cunt, assholes, bastards' filled the air. The expletives and curses hung in the air like a horrible thundercloud. "Goddamit, who did this? You assholes on this quarterdeck know. You had to hear it. Or someone heard it. I want everyone who stood quarterdeck watches last night up here right now! By god, we're getting to the bottom of this ASAP! Get the XO up here on the double!"

He continued to spew and sputter invective as he stormed off the ship to his car. Its passenger side door a sad twist of metal adorned with indentions the size of a human foot. He shouted for the XO to get his ass out there on the double.

Jack walked out and stood silently as the captain continued his rant. Finally came the clincher: "I want the full crew mustered on the pier. Right here. In dress blues with medals. I'm going to inspect their asses and anyone not meeting my expectations is going to be in hack."

"No, fuck it." He had apparently forgotten that the entire crew was *already* in hack, but he recovered quickly. "I'm keeping 'em in hack. You see to it, XO. And in the meantime, I want them turned out on this pier and they're gonna stand here at attention until someone confesses."

"Captain, it's pretty warm for dress blues. Can't we let 'em wear whites? I'm afraid that we may have some people passing out."

"No, godamnit, XO, you fuckin' pussy. Get 'em out here. Officers too. I *want* all of them to pass out."

By 0900, the ship's company was assembled by divisions on the pier, at attention, with their officers in front of their divisions. The XO stood in front of the entire formation. And there they stood. And stood. And stood. Sweat appeared on their foreheads, dripped down their chests and backs, soaked their uniform tops. Sailors began dropping within an hour-and-a-half, and by eleven, as the sun stood almost overhead, forty percent were gone. On deck, the ship's corpsman tried to help them, but there was little he could do. The awful toll mounted with each hour, while Cork sat in his room, smoking a cigar and muttering curses.

Finally, after almost three hours, with noon approaching, Chief Petty Officer Majors, the chief boatswain's mate and master-at-arms, requested permission to address the crew out of presence of the officers. Jack granted it, and he and the other officers went aboard the Black. "You guys listen to me," Chief Majors said. "I'm standin' out here sweatin' because some wise guy kicked in the captain's car and I don't like it one bit. Now whoever did it better confess or when I do find out—and I will find out—I'm going to take a work party and beat the livin' shit outta you. So, save your ass a world class beatin' and come forward."

There was silence. No one came forward. "I mean it, goddamnit. I'm too old for this chicken shit. You better come forward or it's gonna be hell to pay for your ass."

A hand went up. It was Seaman First Class Dale. "What is it, Dale?" Majors asked. "Was it you?"

"Yes Chief. It was me."

"Who else? Did someone help you?"

Dale was silent.

Another hand went up. It was Petty Officer Third Class Ramirez. "Okay, Ramirez, was it you, too?"

"Yeah, Chief. I did it, too."

"Was there anybody else?"

"No, Chief," Dale said. "Just us two."

"You stupid fucks. You got the whole ship three hours out here in the sun and no telling what else."

Majors went onboard the ship where the XO and officers stood and told Jack that two men had confessed. Jack went to the captain's quarters, and the captain ordered the ship's company dismissed. "Send those fuckin' assholes in here," he told Jack. "I want to look them in the fuckin' eyes and ask 'em why they did it."

He did look them in the eyes, and all he got was that they didn't know.

"Court-martial them, XO. Give them a special court martial. And I want six, six and a kick. Do you understand?"

"Yessir, but in accordance with Navy Regs we aren't supposed to interfere in a court martial, Captain. That's probably what will happen but I'm uncomfortable ordering it."

"Goddamit, XO, you're being a fuckin' pussy again. If you won't order it, I will. Put Liam McNamara in charge and Sessums and Tyson on it. And tell McNamara to see me. Now get out!"

The court martial convened, and six-six-and-a-kick is what the two men got. The brig was on the base, and the same Marines who had worked Baucom over still ran it. And ran the prisoners. And ran them. And beat them. And hosed them. Offenses against officers were particularly egregious, so those malfeasants got it the worst, as the officer in charge exacted revenge for this attack on one of his fellow officers. It took only three days to break Dale. Ramirez, tougher, never broke. Then they were gone with their BCD's, just short of a dishonorable discharge, the Navy's career death sentence that would last a lifetime.

Chapter Ten
The Third Cruise

August 1, 1968

The ship, with morale at a new low—and that was a hard thing for Cork to accomplish, but he had—headed south down Tokyo Bay with the usual traffic and Cork's usual reaction to it. The bridge was a Chinese fire drill, and Cork relieved the officer-of-the-deck twice. Jack stood silently over the chart, relaying course corrections to the OOD. Paul Sessums, in CIC, made recommendations as to course and speed changes to accommodate the Rules of the Nautical Road. Cork vetoed nearly every recommendation either of them made and, once again refusing to take the conn, roared his own corrections to Liam McNamara.

That night, he came up with the ultimate humiliation for the crew: a 'short-arm inspection'. He and Jack, whom he didn't trust to do it alone, would conduct it, and all of the officers would accompany them and the corpsman.

They began forward and worked aft. Entering a berthing compartment, Jack would order 'attention on deck', and then each man would be ordered to produce his penis and 'milk it down': squeeze it and move his hand up and down until it either produced discharge or did nothing. Those who produced discharge were put on report, even though there was no support for doing so in Navy Regulations, which specified that—as with sunburn—clap was a sin only if it impaired the sailor's ability to carry out his duties.

Cork didn't care, and the awful toll mounted as the inspection team worked its way aft and then inspected the men then on watch. Forty-six men were found infected, and the ship had penicillin for about five of them. The rest would have to wait for treatment at Cam Ranh Bay. Cork was delighted with his short-arm inspection. His crew was humiliated by it.

One of Cork's rules that the XO had codified in ship's regulations—an extra-judicial compilation that had no known precedent or underpinning in Navy customs, traditions or regulations—was that men must wear their dungaree shirts tucked in at all times, and no facial hair was allowed, even sideburns. The ship's Black sailors, however, liked chin whiskers, while the white sailors were partial to sideburns, so it was Jack's Sisyphean task to ensure that the entire crew complied with Cork's egregious rule. Cork required the crew to muster at quarters—normally an in-port function—each morning at sea. Jack, of course, was to inspect the entire crew and discipline any miscreants, and Cork, if he subsequently observed a violation of his rule, would hold Jack responsible.

It was a sedentary, sunny afternoon on the bridge as the Black steamed in open seas toward Cam Ranh Bay. Cork sat in his captain's chair puffing on a noxious cigar and gazing into the bright blue distance, perhaps dreaming of his redemption from the spate of bad things that had befallen him and the Black.

And then he saw it. All the way forward, a group of six sailors stood with their backs to the bridge and—oh, no! —their shirts were not tucked. Cork, not surprisingly, exploded.

"Who are those men, Mr. McNamara? Are they yours'? Goddamit, they are disobeying a direct order. By God I'm gonna teach them a fuckin' lesson, those goddamn teatheads."

Cork grabbed the ship's bullhorn and began shouting at the men to report to the bridge.

They didn't budge.

He cursed them.

They didn't budge.

"Goddamit, those sonsabitches! Order Mr. Henderson to the bridge! By god he's gonna go down there and find out who these men are."

The Boatswains Mate called for Mr. Henderson to report to the bridge.

He did.

"You get your fuckin' ass down there and put those men on report," Cork barked.

"Aye, sir."

Then the men, without turning to face the bridge, dropped their trousers, bent over, and gave Cork a mooning of the first magnitude. He exploded further, and the men then slipped silently into the forward hatch and into blessed anonymity.

They were never identified, and Cork, out of punishment options, continued to fume and curse.

His executive officer, meanwhile, just drank—in his stateroom, every night. Scotch and warm water from his lavatory spigot. He drank away the pain that haunted him: his marriage to Amanda, his loss of Melanie, his executive officer position on this dreadful ship, the mounting sense of hopelessness that was rising in him. Most days, he didn't shave, and he delegated inspections of messing and berthing. Jack stumbled through each day, just getting by, just going through the motions.

Cam Ranh Bay

August 5, 1968

Her letter was waiting for him when they tied up at Cam Ranh Bay. He opened it and in shock and horror read: "Dear Jack, I lost the baby. I miscarried at a little over four months. I am sick and sorry. Please understand. Love, Amanda."

Jack sat at his desk in stunned silence. There would be no baby. Amanda was no longer pregnant. There was no longer any reason for him to be married to her, but he *was* married to her and he had lost Melanie, and there was no going back for Melanie. *Jesus, what the hell have I done? If we had just waited. Maybe I wouldn't have had to marry Amanda. But how could I have done that? The admiral would have done me in for sure. Oh Jesus. I am trapped and I'm trapped for no reason. And Melanie is gone.*

He wrote Amanda: "I am so sorry to hear that and know that you are saddened by it. I wish I could do something, but I can't. I must soldier on down here and hope that you get over the sadness that I know you feel. Again, I am sorry." He wrote more to tell her about the ship, tell her about Cork and his rules and rants, tell her where they were going. That night he drank himself insensate at the Cam Ranh Navy Officers' Club in an attempt—largely futile—to mitigate the pain that he felt, and then he struggled back to the Black. The pier was slick with diesel, and he slipped and fell and then stumbled up the brow to the quarterdeck, a fuel oil-stained mess. The men on the quarterdeck, headed by Ensign Tyson, looked away, as if to hide his shame. Jack fell into his rack, once again turning into the waves of nausea that rolled in toward him.

They got underway on August 12 and headed north for I Corps. For the next sixty days, they fired almost non-stop at North Vietnam regulars infiltrating South Vietnam through the DMZ in small groups that traveled at night. The heat-seeking plane would fly over and locate them and call-for-fire. The Black would then do her thing, and the fields would be covered with North Vietnamese dead the next morning. The problem for the Black was that the firing missions were called in all night long, so Cork kept them at general quarters all night long. Then, after a two-hour break, they again went to general quarters for the morning call-for-fire and around 1400, they did it again. Exhaustion stalked the Black's decks like the specter of death.

Finally, on October 13, they refueled at Cam Ranh and got underway for the Subic. There they would clean up the ship, get rid of the rust running down her sides, and then head south for the Leyte Gulf Festival in Tacloban, on Leyte Island. Jack took with him a screaming headache from another night at the O Club that savaged his brain.

Tacloban

Jack navigated them down through Surigao Strait, where, 24 years earlier, one branch of the Japanese fleet had attempted to enter Leyte Gulf, only to be met by the great guns of Admiral Oldendorf's squadron of old battleships. It had been a smashing victory. The high green escarpments of Surigao rose out of the water on both sides, and behind them the enormous sun dropped into an emerald sea.

At night, Jack continued to drink warm scotch. He drank after eight o'clock reports to the captain, and after a few stiff ones, he fell into bed and slept.

They arrived at the entrance to Tacloban harbor on October 19, and although Jack could have navigated her in, local regulations required the use of a local pilot. Early on a foggy morning, with the heat boiling off the island of Leyte, the Black tied up at a small wooden pier in the harbor, and the men, dressed in whites, went ashore.

The schedule of events came aboard in the hands of a Seventh Fleet officer, Lieutenant Commander Harry Ferrier, who met them at the pier. There would be a reception and dinner that night for the wardroom of the Black on the

Australian cruiser HMAS Canberra, which would be arriving shortly. The next day would be open for tours of the various World War II battlefields that surrounded the town, and there would be another reception and dinner for the officers at the governor's house. The governor was the brother of Imelda Marcos, the first lady of the Philippines. On the third day, the Black's sailors were to form a platoon—under the command of Ensign Henderson—and march in a parade through downtown Tacloban. The Seventh Fleet band would provide the marching music, as would an Australian band off the Canberra for her sailors in the parade. The Australians, however, would play and march at a slower pace than that of the Black's sailors. This difference would constitute a problem for the American sailors, but there would be another problem that would not inhere to the benefit of Captain Cork, and it—a looming disaster—lay spectrally before them.

Jack had Hinky Henderson take charge of the platoon of sailors who would march in the parade. Henderson worked them twice a day for two days. He assured both the CO and his XO that they were in 'tip-top shape'.

The governor's home was a tropical paradise: wide verandas and stucco and lizards that clung to the ceiling and, with long tongues, nabbed insects that circled the overhead light fixtures. But the real bonus for Jack and the Black's wardroom was the two Peace Corps workers who attended. Susan Sullivan from Sioux Falls, South Dakota was a fairly good-looking girl, with a great body, and she wore a short skirt that displayed her legs well. The other Peace Corps worker was Sally Harkins from the University of Maine, smaller than Sue and prettier, also.

Jack went after Sally first. "You're from Maine. I dated a girl in Newport last summer who was from the University of Maine. Her name was Nancy Reimers. Ever run across her?"

Sally smiled. "No. Never. But I'm glad to run across you. I haven't seen an American man in two years. It's good to see one now, especially a handsome one in a handsome uniform."

"Thanks, Sally. These dress whites *are* a good-looking uniform. We don't wear them very often but I'm happy when we do."

"What do you do on the Black River?"

"I'm executive officer."

"Where are you from Mr. Executive Officer of the Black River?"

"Mississippi, but I've been in the Navy the last three years and been all over but Mississippi's still home, I guess."

They talked and drank and talked and drank some more. "Jack, I've got an apartment on the side of a home not that far away from here. Do you want to come to my place for a cold beer and a visit?"

"Yes, absolutely. You ready to go?"

"I'm ready."

They walked down the pot-holed street. Overhead, in the faint light of the street lamps, large insects circled in an endless dance that drew them ever closer to an incandescent death. Behind them, at the governor's house, the sound of faint music played by a small Filipino band drifted up the road after them.

They walked on.

Her apartment, as advertised, was on the side of a large two-story white frame house, and it had a side entrance of its own. Inside, they sat on a couch and drank cold San Miguel beer and smoked his Marlboro cigarettes that she had been unable to buy in Tacloban. And then she got up and came to him and straddled him and pressed against him. She kissed him hard, and they made love. Jack drank another San Miguel and then returned to the party. He drank three more scotches and then went back to the Black and took off his uniform and fell into a drunken sleep, turning frequently into the waves of dizziness that once again rolled toward him.

Melanie

It was another early autumn that year, and as October came, smoke from burning leaves hung heavily above the town, and students in bell-bottom pants and floppy shirts now, made their way to classes. Melanie had moved in with Mark Goldberg at his house on Old Chapel Hill Road. Her attire, too, had changed to a hippie look, with long loose skirts and baggy blouses. Now that it was cooler, she wore clunky shoes, almost like the Boondockers Jack had worn in his days there.

"Want me to roll you an MJ cigarette?" Mark asked her. There was music on the radio, and Melanie read by a gas space heater that cast an orange glow onto the floor where she sat cross-legged. The music had changed dramatically in only a year, from Motown to 'Here's to You Mrs. Robinson' and 'Stoned

Soul Picnic'. Gone, too, were the equable college clothes of the earlier sixties, replaced now by equally equable hippie attire, and some of the males wore ponytails.

"Yes," she said. "I'll have one. It'll help me concentrate on this Shakespeare. Whatta you think your schedule is for finishing your masters? I'm looking at the end of next summer."

"Jesus, two years to do a masters?"

"Yeah. I thought I could do it by this summer but I've kinda lost interest in it. I'm gonna cut back on my course load and try to figure out what I want to do my dissertation on. I'm really just sick of it."

"You're still grieving losing Jack, aren't you?"

"No, not really. The whole thing just floored me. It took my enthusiasm for school away. It's not that I'm still in love with Jack at all. No, what I feel for Jack is nothing but hatred and anger. And you were there for me and I want to be with you now. I just don't want to go to school. I guess I'll go on and get my masters and then take some time off and see if I want to go on and get a PHD."

"I tell you what, girl. Let's go on and get married. That'll make you feel better. I mean, we're living together and there's no reason not to. I love you and you love me so let's do it."

"Oh, what the hell. Okay. Let's do it."

The Tacloban Death March

Ensign Henderson had the Black's marching platoon in great shape to march in the parade. They would directly precede the Seventh Fleet band and follow the Australian band, which would follow the Aussie sailors. It seemed so simple in theory; in practice it would be something else, for, after all, every one of them knew that sailors don't know, or care to learn, how to march.

As the sailors waited in line, some of the Aussies called to them. "Come on over here, swabbies. We got something for you."

The Canberra sailors stood on the porch of a bar, and they were swigging cold San Miguel beer. "Come on guys, have a beer with us."

Henderson: "Don't do that. You're on duty. Stay where you are."

"Fuck this shit," Boatswains Mate Second Class Roberts said. "I want a cold one, too."

He broke ranks and headed for the bar. The whole platoon followed. They did not fear Henderson, who according to Cork, was a 'whip sock'.

The parade took an hour or so to get started, and by then, the Black's sailors had consumed several cold San Miguels. Henderson had decided to have a couple himself. They would sweat the alcohol out, Radioman Second Class Bartholomew said. It would not be a problem.

The Aussies fell into formation and started out with their band playing behind them. Then came the Black's platoon, with Hinky Henderson carrying a sword in front of his face in the 'salute' position. The Seventh Fleet band cranked up behind them with 'Stars and Stripes Forever', and they were underway. Heat rose from the pavement, and the sun beat on them like a gas furnace sitting on each man's shoulders. Sweat poured from their faces, and the San Miguels roiled their guts. Some of them belched, and all of them wobbled. A faint miasma of disaster arose from their ranks.

Encouraged by two conflicting beats from two different bands, the Black's sailors marched hesitantly forward. Then came a turn onto Main Street. "Column left, march!" Henderson called out. He made the turn. The others tried to make it, too, but the combination of heat and sweat and beer decimated their ranks. A few men drifted off into the crowd, a few stumbled and almost fell.

By then, they were in full view of the crowd that lined both sides of Main Street. Ensign Henderson was particularly hard hit by the beer. He wove a winding path from side to side in the street. Some of the sailors tried to keep time with the Stars and Stripes, others with the Aussies. All of them bobbed and weaved about the street.

Cork was on the reviewing stand. He saw the Aussies coming, smartly in step and marching crisply. They were accustomed to alcohol. They had it on their ship. Plus, they had but one band with which to keep time. That band followed, also crisp and marching in step with their sailors ahead. The Black's platoon followed the Aussies. It was a confused mishmash, out of step, with the front half of the platoon marching in slow step with the Aussie band and the rear half marching in a quicker step to the Seventh Fleet band and stepping on the heels of the front half of the platoon, who stumbled forward, as some of their shoes came off. Cork looked on in horror as Henderson wobbled from side to side, and the platoon of sailors disintegrated into a roiling mass of men bumbling forward, while their leader continued shuffling from one side of the street to the other.

"Goddamit, what the hell's wrong with those pukes?" Cork muttered, as terror rose into his face. "Goddamit men, get in step," he muttered sibilantly. "What in the hell is going on here?"

The Seventh Fleet officer stood beside him. Through gritted teeth he groaned and said, "This is the worst thing I've ever seen. You've managed not only to embarrass yourself and your ship, you've managed to embarrass the whole Navy and the entire country. Good god man! What the hell are your people doing? Jesus."

The sorry spectacle continued past the reviewing stand, as the island governor, the Tacloban mayor, their wives and other dignitaries laughed wildly at the disaster that was unfolding before their eyes. From the crowd standing along the street, there arose a murmur and then a soft laugh and then a loud laugh that turned into a roar as the crowd pointed and howled.

Then it happened. Boyd Tyce, a backsliding Baptist from Bettendorf, Iowa, who was prone to savage bouts of seasickness, stumbled into the crowd on the far side of the street and threw up his breakfast and the three San Magoos he had ingested before the Death March. Onlookers scattered. Others laughed. Cork, however, did not laugh. He stormed across the street and confronted the sick Buntin. "Goddamit, Buntin. You fuckin' teathead. What the fuck's wrong with you, man?"

Buntin, bending over now with the dry heaves, raised his head lugubriously and said, "I'm sorry, Captain..." and then he puked on Cork's Delos-Reyes-new-polish job. Cork jumped like a Mississippi bullfrog, and a stream of profanity spewed from his mouth like the puke from Tyce's mouth. Cork then returned to the reviewing stand. The Seventh Fleet liaison officer, Lieutenant Commander Ferrier, confronted him.

"Lieutenant Commander Cork, I'm going to report this to Admiral Kitchings and I'm sure he'll take it down the chain of command to your Commodore. You better buckle up and hold on tight because this is going to be a major brouhaha for you and your command. You understand?"

Cork, devastated by what he had just seen, merely nodded, and with the Black's platoon now past the reviewing stand, the men tried to march on, as sorry looking from the rear as they had been from the front and sides.

The other members of the Black's wardroom stood silently and despondently as the platoon disintegrated before them like confetti in a breeze. "Jesus," Jack said. "We better stand damn by. The captain is going to have our collective ass on this one." And Cork was. And he did.

At Cam Ranh Bay, Cork ordered the crew and officers into dress whites and then ashore in formation. Jack, he ordered, was to wear a sword. "XO, godamnit, I want you to march these fuckin' teatheads until they drop. And I want them looking four dot oh. I mean A-plus-plus. You got it?"

"Yessir, Captain. Four dot oh."

Cork eyed him suspiciously in an effort to see if he was mocking him and then left for the Officers' Club. It was a savagely hot, terribly humid Vietnam afternoon when they began marching around the base, winding on the sorry dusty streets by barracks and the BOQ and the swift boat staff headquarters and the base commander's headquarters then out onto the field that served both the baseball teams and the flag football teams. They marched on. The sun beat down on them mercilessly. Cork was nowhere to be seen. Jack led the parade. Liam McNamara and Hinky Henderson led the Weapons-Deck Division. Paul Sessums and T. P. Burwell, a sweating walrus, led Operations, and Bob Tyson, another sweating walrus, led Engineering. Dave Duvall the Supply Officer, followed with his three sailors in a desultory manner, his slumping drink-of-water body heavy with pathos.

They marched from 1300 to 1600, sweating and wetting their clean, pressed whites. The sun reddened their faces, and on the athletic field, dust rose up and choked them. Jack called cadence: "Hup, two, three four. Your left, your left, your left, right, left, right. Hup! Hup! Hup, two, three, four. Hup!" He took them through column lefts and column rights, through left and right flanking movements, through "to the rear, march!" And they did it. And they did it right. And on and on it went. And the sweat poured down their faces and down their chests, and Jack marched them on, into despair and disbelief and what ultimately would be into darkness.

Melanie

She sat on the floor smoking a reefer and drinking cheap wine—Mogen David. "What're you going to do, Mark, now that you've got your draft notice?" she asked.

"I fucking don't know. I want to finish my masters here and then I could go to Canada like some of my friends have but if I go now, it will fuck everything up. My masters, my life with you, my life, period. If I did go, would you come with me?"

"No, I'm like you. I want to finish my masters and I will finish my course work this fall semester and then work on my thesis next semester and finish it by summer. I would come then."

"Well, I tell you what, Miss Priss. You've let me know where I stand with you and it's not very high on your totem pole."

"Well, I married you, didn't I, Mr. Mark Goldberg? Doesn't that say a lot about where you stand?"

"Would you go to Canada if it were Jack? I bet you would have. I know you don't love me like you loved him, do you?"

"I love you enough to marry you and I didn't marry Jack, did I? You go on to Canada and get settled and I'll come up there next summer. It's not the end of the world. I'll come up there Christmas holidays and again in the spring and then move up there next summer and teach."

"Tell you what I'm going to do. I'm going to stay here and tough it out as long as I can. At least try to finish this semester. There's a rumor that they may eliminate the draft and go to a lottery system. If that's the case, then maybe I'll get out of it all together."

"Yeah, I've heard that one, too. But my understanding is if they do it, it won't be until sometime next year. Well, what the hell? Take your chances. The odds are they won't come arrest you. They've got people all over the country refusing to report. Heck, Muhammed Ali refused to report. Go for it!"

Chapter Eleven
Back to the Gunline

They left Cam Ranh Bay after a brutal rocket loadout that the captain had personally overseen. He had shouted orders at them to speed up and had gotten in the ear of any man he thought was a 'slacker'. He had the officers—including the XO—in the line, and he shouted at them by name to 'pick it up'. The loadout took almost three hours, and the officers, unaccustomed to the sun and the effort required to move the rockets along the line, suffered terribly. Then, with no swim call, they were underway for the Mekong Delta.

Their first firing mission came on a muzzy morning with mists rising off the fetid waters of the delta. The airborne spotter wanted multiple rocket launchers to fire beyond the range of the Black's longest-range rockets.

Cork rang CIC. "XO, get up here! I want you to take us in."

Jack reported to the bridge. "In where, sir?"

"Into the delta. We ought to be able to push up through the reeds in there and pick up a few hundred yards and reach his targets."

"Sir, I don't recommend that. We don't have any information on the depths in there and the only thing we can do is rely on a lead line. The problem with that is that the reeds are going to impede the lead from sinking to the bottom so we aren't going to know how much water we have below the keel."

"Goddamit, XO! Doesn't anybody on this ship have any confidence and competence? I can fuckin' handle it. So, get to it, mister navigator."

"Aye, aye sir. Will you take the conn?"

"No. Mr. McNamara will take her in. Won't you Mr. McNamara?"

"Sir," Liam said, "I feel like we're making a mistake and I don't want to have the conn if we run aground."

"Well, who the fuck is going to take her in, Mr. McNamara?"

"I guess you will, sir."

"Fuck I won't. I'm in command of this ship and you will damn well do what I say. You hear me mister?"

"Yessir." McNamara turned to the voice tube to the pilot house. "Enter in the log that I am taking the conn under protest, Boats, and that I do not recommend entering the delta."

Jack was next. "Boats, also enter in the log that the XO does not recommend entering the delta."

"Aye, sir. Mr. McNamara is taking the conn under protest and does not recommend entering the delta. And the XO doesn't either."

"Very well, Boats." McNamara turned to Cork. "What's your pleasure, sir?"

"I'm gonna remember this, you pukes. Okay, Mr. McNamara, take her in slowly. Get a lead-line man up on the bow and a sound-powered phone operator to relay his depth readings. We're going the hell in."

They turned and moved toward the reeds that formed the edge of the delta. As they approached the lead lineman began sending depth readings up to the bridge. Two fathoms—twelve feet. Ten feet and on down. The ship, fully loaded as she was, drew six feet, so they had only four feet to work with. And that gradually diminished as they reached the reeds. "Keep going, Mr. McNamara. You got a couple of feet to work with."

"Aye, sir. Rivera, tell him I want those readings as fast as he can get them."

They inched ahead. The reeds parted as though for the baby Moses.

Then, the lead lineman reported that he could not get the lead to sink.

"Keep going," Cork said. "XO, how far are we from target?"

"Captain, I can't tell you that. There's nothing to navigate by. It's all just flat and reedy. We're in uncharted territory here."

"Keep moving ahead Mr. McNamara. We ought to be close to our longest range. XO, go below and take charge of firing. Get the spotter to give you coordinates and let's start putting some heat on their yellow asses."

Jack went below, as the ship edged ahead. The spotter called for fire, but Wallis could not calculate the range and firing azimuth, because he did not know where they were. It didn't matter. Suddenly, there was a gut-gouging scraping sound followed by a *thud* followed by a shudder that shook the Black from bow to stern. Men all over the ship slammed forward, against steel bulkheads, fell onto steel decks.

"Goddamit, Mr. McNamara," Cork said, suddenly stuttering and straining to spit out the words through a tightening jaw and an even tighter throat. "What's wrong?" he croaked. "What's going on? We're not moving?"

"Sir, I think we're aground." Into the voice tube, Liam spoke calmly, "Boats, enter in the log that the ship ran aground at ten-twenty-seven."

"Aye sir," the Boatswain intoned. "The ship is aground at ten-twenty-seven."

"No, godammit, don't you enter shit into that log," Cork croaked. "We're not aground. We're just resting. All engines back full."

"All engines back full!" Liam McNamara shouted into the voice tube.

The ship shook as the twin screws dug in. It shook more as the Black strained against the muddy bottom into which she had slammed and was now lodged.

The Black did not budge. Cork screamed his usual litany of profanity and bolted from wing to wing, looking at nothing but reeds with wild eyes suffused with terror. He ordered Jack to the bridge.

"Godammit, Mr. McNamara, what the fuck? Can't you do anything?"

"No sir. There's nothing I can do. The engines either will pull us out or they won't. And it looks like they won't."

"XO, what about you? Can you get us out of here?"

"Sir, I'm with Mr. McNamara. There is nothing I know of that we can do."

"Lot of help you are, you teatheads. All right, have Mr. Sessums call for someone to come get us out of this mess."

"Who do you have in mind, Captain?" Liam asked.

"Go on fleet common and find out who's in the neighborhood," the captain said.

Liam McNamara relayed the command down to Paul Sessums in CIC, and later that day an ocean-going tug—the one they had seen at Phu Quoc Island—arrived to extricate the Black.

Cork had retired to his stateroom and did not return to the bridge that day.

They remained on the line for the next two months, firing every day, punctuated only by trips back to Cam Ranh Bay, as though the Commodore was punishing them for their failure in Refresher Training and in Tacloban. It was brutal. Cork continued his rampages, accusing his officers, including his XO, of various forms of malfeasance, misfeasance, and nonfeasance relating to duties that no one understood or even knew existed, other than to recognize them as functions of Cork's fevered brain.

Thanksgiving and Christmas came, both national holidays and both specified as such by Navy Regulations. Cork, however, had other ideas. He ordered a full workday around two firing missions, and he sat on the bridge and glowered while on deck, Henderson's men mindlessly chipped paint, and the gunners mates serviced the rocket launchers. Below, Ensign Tyson's men cleaned the bilges—the dirtiest work of all—and in the wardroom, Delos Reyes polished silver and shoes. It was business as usual aboard the Black.

Jack went to the captain. "Sir, we'd like to hold a cookout on deck. We have a couple of grills and we cook steaks and hamburgers on them, we being the officers. The men love the food and they love having the officers cook it. Is that okay with you?"

"Fuck no; it's not okay with me. These assholes have done nothing to deserve it and they're not going to get it. Do you understand, XO?"

"Yes sir. I understand. We'll shitcan the idea."

In the wardroom, the days passed slowly. Jack took reports from his department heads and reported the ship 'all secure' each night at 2000 to the captain. From Cork, he received a hodgepodge of complaints and orders. The gravamen of his complaints was that Jack was too easy on the officers and the crew, that the ship was a slipshod operation, and that it was all Jack's fault. "Godammit, XO, I want this ship squared away, bow to stern. I see men all the time with their shirts not tucked and sometimes they are slow getting to general quarters. That's on you, XO, and it's going to show up in your next fitness report. Do you understand?"

"Yessir, I understand and I'll try harder to get the ship in the shape that you want."

"I'm cursed. I got a wardroom full of fucking teatheads and an XO who doesn't seem to give a shit. And I got a crew that can't shoot rockets or the five-inch gun worth a shit. Damn McNamara! He's going to pay, too, come fitness report time. The only one of them that doesn't stay in trouble is Dave Duvall and that's because he doesn't have shit to do."

Filled with Cork's anger and threats, the days ground painfully on. Cork had the crew at general quarters two times during the day and once at night. Fatigue blanketed the ship like a stink, and with personnel inspections every morning, morale sank deeper into the toilet.

For Jack, it was more of the same: loudspeaker calls for the XO to report here, there, topside, below decks, to the wardroom, to the captain's cabin, to engineering, gunnery, the ship's admin office, everywhere, nowhere. Cork followed up Jack's inspection of messing and berthing with his own, and for every speck of dust he found, every rack not made to Naval Officer' Candidate School standards, he called the XO to report to the offending place on the ship and make it right.

Because of Cork's explosion after what was known as 'the full house hand', the officers could no longer play cards. So, they watched movies, the best of which was '2001: A Space Odyssey'. And they slept whenever they could. The ten-hour workdays, coupled with general quarters at night, wore them down, while Cork slept during nighttime firing and took long naps in the late morning and early afternoon between firing missions. Mercifully, he took most of his meals in his stateroom now, so Jack presided over quiet meals peopled with hollow-eyed officers. Cork had them by the short ones now, and there was, and would be, no relief.

Melanie

They sat in her living room, heavy now with pot smoke. Melanie was starting down off a major high. She looked at Mark. He was supine on the floor with his head in her lap. "Oh, my god," he whispered sibilantly. "This stuff is amazing. You've got to try it, Melanie."

"I don't want to. Pot is enough for me."

"Aww, fuck pot. This is the way to go. Here, tear off a piece of this blotter. Just put it on your tongue. It'll dissolve and, in a minute, you'll experience the most amazing high ever. It'll make pot look like child's play. Come on, Melanie. What have you got to lose?"

She didn't want to fight with Mark again. Ever since he had started using LSD, he had been different. Not cool toward her or anything like that, just more zombie-like. He seemed to go from high to high. She didn't like it, and she had complained to him about it. He shrugged it off: "Oh, screw it," he would say. "It's just LSD."

"Oh, for god's sake, Mark. Okay. If it's that damn important to you, I'll take it. But just this once. Okay?"

"Okay. Here's a tab."

She took it, and within minutes, she knew she had found her god.

Chapter Twelve
The Investigation

The New Year came, and it would not take long for the Black to enter the annals of Navy lore. She had fired up and down the coast of South Vietnam, and the mishaps continued. The Black's rockets seldom found the target, and the five-inch gun, to which Cork resorted in frustration, proved worse. The 'Top Gun' on the gunline was a floating, firing disaster, and Cork reacted in predictable fashion: refusing to let the crew go ashore in Cam Ranh, once again requiring them to stand inspection in dress whites every morning, requiring attendance at church services, which he had Dave Duvall conduct, and continuing to extend the work day two hours, which was contrary to Navy Regulations. Word about the Black's inaccuracy was not long in reaching Yokosuka.

The sailor who had been raped in Hong Kong—Seaman Francis—was cleaning the athwart-ship's passageway. As he wiped down the exterior of the bulkhead that formed the outer wall of Cork's cabin, he saw a hole in the bulkhead. He peered through it. He would later say that he saw something. Something big. Something bad. "It was Captain Cork." In Francis's own words, Cork was "abusing himself."

Mail went out on an underway replenishment ship. Then, a couple of weeks later, a top-secret message arrived from the Commodore in Yokosuka: "Depart gunline immediately and proceed Subic at top speed. Notify originator of ETA. An investigative officer—Captain William A. Thomas—will meet you."

Paul Sessums passed the message along to Jack, who took it to Cork.

"Okay," Cork said softly. "I don't know what this is about but let's head to Subic at twelve knots. Calculate an ETA, XO, and pass it along to the staff." Then he was quiet.

Jack actually felt sorry for him. Cork seemed shattered, and it showed in everything he did. Or didn't do. He continued to take all of his meals in this cabin. Rarely came to the bridge. Calls to the XO ceased. As a result, Jack took over the ship. He had quit drinking in his stateroom, and he navigated by the stars at morning and evening twilight. He met each morning with the officers to discuss the coming day and their approaching arrival in Subic. The ghost of Bill Stockwell floated throughout the ship.

They arrived on January 18, 1969, and Captain Thomas and a coterie of two full lieutenants and four chief petty officers were there to meet them. They came aboard immediately and locked down the ship: no one was to leave or come aboard, other than the investigative team. Interviews commenced that afternoon, starting with Captain Thomas interviewing the CO and the XO and the two lieutenants with the rest of the wardroom. The chiefs fanned out and interviewed the sailors. The process took three days. Then they left, and Cork granted liberty to the crew.

The Black remained in Subic for a week, and on January 28, got underway for the gunline. Jack navigated the ship across the South China Sea, oversaw the ammo loadout, and then took the Black around the horn of South Vietnam and up the west coast of IV Corps, the steaming, festering Mekong Delta.

The CO stayed in his stateroom, and the ship was quiet. Cork, now silent and alone, acquiesced when Jack asked to put the men in shorts and tee shirts, when he requested permission to let the night watches fire H and I, did away with the morning inspections, cut the workday to Navy Regulation 0800 to 1630. Firing became crisp and accurate. The crew was its old Bill Stockwell-commanded self: confident and competent. The Black worked like the Boston Celtics played basketball: perfectly. Jack, needed by his ship now, was his old self. He navigated the Black along the coast of Vietnam, called the ship to general quarters, and oversaw firing on the bridge.

Melanie

She had finished her master's coursework in December of 1968 and had begun work on her dissertation. It was a feckless effort. She was burned out on school and was hung-over most days from drugs, wine and the Doors. Her drug regimen started with pot and wine, capped with a dose of LSD. She used, and she slept, and sometimes she worked on her dissertation.

Mark finally confronted her one night at dinner: "Melanie, I've been watching you for several weeks now and I have to say something. I'm really concerned with your using. You are hitting it hard every night and I'm worried that you are getting hooked on getting high and I'm worried about you."

She sat and looked beyond him in an alcohol and pot-induced haze.

"Well, what the hell, Mark? You use, too. And you got me started on LSD, didn't you? And now you're mister self-righteous? Jesus. Give me a break."

"I don't use every night and I don't use LSD but once a week now, if that. You're hitting the wine and the pot and the LSD hard every night. You're not doing shit on your dissertation and you never want to do anything anymore but sit at home and use and I am damn worried about you."

"Screw you, bastard. I can handle it and I damn sure don't need you of all people to tell me what to do." She got up and walked into their bedroom and slammed the door. Mark shook his head sadly.

Report of the Investigation

The notice came on February 20 in a 'flash' encrypted message from the command that had conducted the investigation. It was followed by another flash message from the Commodore ordering the Black to return to Subic, where it would be met by the Commodore's chief of staff, Commander Bill Campbell.

The investigative results were presented as 'findings of fact' and 'conclusions of the investigating officer', which were just that: the conclusions that he had drawn based on the facts he had found. The investigating officer found that it was likely that Cork had masturbated and had been seen by a crew member, the damaged Seaman Francis. He found that Cork had abused his position of authority by canceling liberty on multiple occasions over minor infractions by only a few—in one case, only two—crew members.

In addition, Cork, the investigating officer concluded, had placed the ship in danger by his inept ship handling that ran the Black aground and had overruled the officer-of-the-deck and the navigator repeatedly without taking the conn—in other words, without taking formal responsibility—a violation of Navy Regulations. The report recited the Black's poor parade performance in Tacloban and set forth details of the Black's ineptitude on the gunline. Other infractions included extending the work day by two hours, implementing mandatory church services, failing to observe holidays mandated by Navy Regs, requiring personnel inspections every morning, requiring the crew to wear dress uniforms for those inspections and even 'excessive cursing at personnel'.

The investigating team gigged him for making the crew stand at attention in the aftermath of Cork's kicked car and for forcing them to march in dress whites at Cam Ranh Bay after the Tacloban disaster. The investigating officer reprimanded Cork for running his ship into the LST the first time he got the Black underway and for ordering the boatswain's mate of the watch not to record either that incident or running the Black aground in the Mekong Delta. Finally, and most importantly, the investigating officer found that Cork had himself fired into a boat of Vietnamese civilians, when the proper action would have been to continue to fire in front of them and have a boarding party inspect their boat for explosives. The inspecting officer stated that he would refer that incident to Commander Seventh Fleet for consideration of a general court martial upon further investigation. Taken together, the investigative report was a searing, damning indictment of Cork and his command.

T. P. Burwell was the first officer to read the second message, and he took it to Paul Sessums who brought it to Jack. "Holy shit," Jack said as he read it. "Jesus, Paul. They've nailed his ass."

"Sure have, XO, and if you'll excuse me for saying it, it couldn't happen to a guiltier guy. I just wonder how he got away with all of this stuff this long."

"Well, I'm not going to get into all of that. It is what it is, as my old history professor at UNC used to say. There is nothing you or I can do about it except tell the CO and let him deal with it. I guess they'll be waiting on the pier for him in Subic and it'll be Katy fucking bar the door."

"Well, I'm glad I don't have your job," Sessums said. "I wouldn't want to have to give him this message."

Jack left his stateroom and climbed down the ladder to the CO's cabin. He knocked and then entered. Cork sat at his desk, fiddling with paperwork and smoking a cigar.

"What is it, XO?"

"Sir, we've got a message from the Commodore about the investigation."

"Well, don't just stand there. What does it say?"

"I think you'd better read it, sir."

Cork snatched the two sheets of paper away from Jack and began to read. As he did the color drained from his already-whiter-than-white face, and his jaw tightened. But he said nothing until finally: "Who has read this, XO?"

"All I know of is Mr. Sessums and I but I would guess that the radioman on duty and probably Mr. Burwell read it, too."

"Get out!"

"Aye, Sir. And Captain, I'm sorry."

"I don't give a fat fuck what you or the rest of this crew of incompetent, disloyal assholes are. Just get the fuck out of my cabin."

"Aye, Sir. The Comphibron Eleven message orders us to Subic. Shall I set a course for Subic, sir?"

"Yes," Cork said despondently. "Take us back."

Jack turned and left, closing the door very softly, as though out of respect for the wounded Cork. He went to the pilot house and laid out the course back to Subic Bay.

That evening Cork, once again, did not come to the wardroom for supper. He rang on the sound-powered phone—a furious screech of a ring—and ordered Delos Reyes to bring his food to him. Delos Reyes returned to the wardroom obviously shaken.

"What happened, Delos Reyes?"

"He was sitting at his desk. Didn't say anything. I set the tray on his desk. He didn't even look up."

"What does he usually do when you take his food in?"

"He usually jumps me about something. His shoes not shined right. His rack not made tight enough. Something. Always something. And he always calls me Cockroach. This time he didn't say anything. Just sat there."

"Okay, Delos Reyes. Stay out of his way as much as possible. Guys you do the same. Let me deal with him if there is any dealing to be done."

They watched 'Cool Hand Luke' in the wardroom, and Jack turned in about 2200. Liam McNamara awakened him shortly after midnight.

"XO, wake up."

"Ok, Liam. What's up? They need me on the bridge?"

"No sir. I need to report something to you," he said gravely.

"What?" Jack sat up in his rack and swung his feet to the deck.

"Captain Cork ordered the master-at-arms, Chief Majors, to bring him a fully loaded forty-five automatic pistols to his stateroom a few minutes ago."

"Jesus," was all Jack said. Then he was quiet while he evaluated this information. Finally, "Has Majors taken the gun to him?"

"Yes sir. Just did. Said Cork is just sitting on his rack in his dress blues with medals and his sword in his lap. You reckon he plans to shoot someone?"

"Dress blues? In this heat? Jesus, Liam. I don't know what he's planning to do. The gun is scary. I hope he doesn't shoot himself." Liam laughed.

"I just hope he doesn't shoot one of us," McNamara said. He turned to leave. Opened the door to the XO's stateroom.

The explosion came then. It rolled through the superstructure, through CIC, up into the pilot house, up and out onto the bridge. Jack's sound-powered phone lit up like a hotplate. He didn't answer and instead bolted for his stateroom door and then down the ladder one level and into the captain's quarters.

It was a horrible mess: Cork's brains slid down the bulkhead next to his bed. Cork himself, his eyes wide and insensate, had fallen back against the same bulkhead, the forty-five on the deck where it had fallen after the shot that he had fired from beneath his mouth into his skull.

"Jesus," Jack said.

"Oh, my god," Liam McNamara said.

A radioman came out of the radio shack and looked in. He threw up in the passageway. CIC emptied into the passageway. Liam McNamara sent them back to their stations.

"Liam, close the door and put a guard out there. I've got to get a message off to the Comphibron Eleven staff in Yokosuka about what has happened. This is a fucking disaster. And I feel fucking terrible."

"Well, you shouldn't, XO. It's not your fault. Not anything you did. Or any of us. Captain brought this on himself. And he fired that gun. Not you. Not us."

Jack returned to his stateroom and drafted a message to the Commodore in Yokosuka. "Captain Cork has taken his own life. Body on board. Ship already enroute Subic. Request instructions." He gave them the ship's position, course, speed and then signed it, 'XO'.

"Send it flash, Ortiz. Top Secret."

"Aye, XO."

The duty officer on the staff in Yokosuka took the message and immediately dispatched an orderly to the Commodore's quarters, as well as to the chief of staff.

Forty minutes later, came the reply. "XO take command. Proceed Subic at top speed. Report position, course and speed every four hours. Upon arrival,

Subic tie up Pier Two. Staff officers will meet the ship. Will notify Subic Base Staff to prepare to remove body. Acknowledge."

Jack replied affirmatively, and he increased speed to twelve knots, the Black's maximum cruising speed. They headed east, across the dark, haunting expanse that was the South China Sea, toward the unknown.

Jack sat in his stateroom smoking over a cup of steaming black Navy coffee. There was a knock.

"Hi, Liam. I guess I'm going to be in command so I need an XO. You are second to me in seniority. Want the job?"

"Yessir, XO, I mean, Captain. I do."

"Very well. You got it. I'll get with you later to transfer everything to you and you inform Hinky Henderson that he's the new weapons officer. Okay?"

"Aye, sir. Will do. But there's one more thing. The captain's body. We got to do something with it before it starts to decompose. If we don't it not only will stink up the ship, it may fall apart when they come to get it in Subic. The corpsman says it is going to happen pretty quickly."

"I agree. Whatta you suggest?"

"We have several body bags that we took aboard during the deal in Hue. We can put him in one of those."

"Good. We can also put him in the reefer and keep him cold. That should slow down decomposition. Make arrangements with Dave Duvall on that."

"Aye, sir. Will do. And XO, I mean skipper. Thanks for giving me the chance."

"You're welcome, Liam. We'll get together on the bridge this afternoon and I'll turn over navigation to you. We'll shoot stars together this evening and then tomorrow you'll be on your own, although I'm always right here if you need me."

McNamara looked at his new CO. The redness that had streaked his eyes was gone now after a month in actual command. His voice was full, rich with energy. Liam McNamara smiled at him. Jack smiled back.

McNamara turned to go.

"One more thing, Liam. Get a working party together under Dave Duvall to clean up the mess in the captain's stateroom. Delos Reyes can head it up."

"Are you going to move in there, skipper?"

"Hell, no. I don't want any part of that place. The memory of the captain with his brains sliding down the bulkhead is too much for me."

"Aye, sir. I understand. We'll get it cleaned up."

Subic Bay

Jack had his new XO navigate her in at Subic, and Ensign Henderson took the conn until they were making their final approach to the pier. Jack took the conn then and pulled her uneventfully alongside the pier. There stood Commodore Brunini's chief of staff, Commander Bill Campbell, and two other staff officers: Lieutenant Commander Carl Butts and Lieutenant Thomas Fischer. As soon as the brow was down, they came aboard and into the wardroom, where Jack joined them.

"Where's the body?" Bill Campbell asked.

"In the reefer, in a body bag," Jack replied.

"Well, I've arranged for a party from the base to come over and collect it. They'll get it embalmed and we'll fly it back with us to Yokosuka and then send it back to the States."

He paused and shook his head sadly. "I tell you what, Jack. I've been in this man's Navy for twenty-six years and I've never seen or heard of anything like this happening. Tell me step-by-step what happened."

Jack walked them through it. He concluded: "Does Elizabeth Cork know?"

"Yes, we sent Byron over to tell her. She's outta her head, as you can imagine. We'll have to see where she wants the body shipped in the States and arrange to get her back. It's a horrible situation. I feel so sorry for her. The other wives are staying with her in shifts. It's not enough—nothing is enough—but it's better than nothing."

Bill Campbell paused, stared into nothing. Shook his head sadly. Then he looked at Jack.

"Well, you're in command now. We'll fleet you up to Lieutenant Commander retroactive to Cork's suicide and you'll have to bring her home. You up to that? If you'd prefer, I can have Carl here do it. He's had command at sea."

"No problem, Commander. I brought her over here and I can take her home. I've done it multiple times with Captain Cork including underway training and I can do it in my sleep. It won't be a problem and I'd like to do it."

"Very well. We'll collect the body. You plan to stay here for a few days, and if you'd like, we'll let you stop in Hong Kong or Taiwan on the way home. Which do you prefer?"

"Sir, I think the crew would prefer—after this especially—just to go home. We've been away several months now and it would probably be better if we went on back to Yoko."

"Very well, Jack. In the meantime, give your men some liberty. We're staying at the BOQ and will head on over there. Can you and your officers have dinner with us at the O Club tonight?"

"Absolutely, sir. That will be nice." He paused, then: "You know, as long as Captain Cork was aboard, I never had dinner with him off the ship but once—at the Chief's Club—and that was a nightmare. Frankly, sir, he had quit coming to dinner with us in the wardroom after the investigation and I never saw him on the bridge again. He didn't even come up for general quarters. I had to move from CIC to the bridge to oversee firing. But we got it done."

"And got it done well, I would say. The people ashore gave you excellent marks the last month. Seems like you turned it around."

"It was a group effort, Commander. All of our officers and petty officers are to be commended."

"I would like to address them in person if you'll allow it and tell them how well they've done and what a tragedy this is. But they need to know that they must carry on."

"Allow it? Heck, I'd love it sir. Tomorrow morning at muster?"

"I'll be here."

The staff team departed, and Jack immediately sounded liberty call. His Sisyphean ordeal had ended.

Melanie

Spring had at last come to the Carolina piedmont, and Chapel Hill was alive with dogwoods standing alone and startling white under the canopy of the large old trees that were everywhere in the town. Melanie sat in the sun and felt its warm rays on her face. She had quit using LSD and had cut far down on her marijuana use and in the amount of wine she drank.

Jack. That sonofabitch. No one has ever done anything like that to me. No one. Ever. I hope to God that he hates his life. I pray to God that he hates being married to that bitch he knocked up. I guess they have a child by now. I wonder how he is as a father. I can't imagine him as a father. Maybe he's great. Maybe he isn't. I shouldn't care. I don't care. I really don't care. I want to hurt him. I'm going to let him know that my life is great and that I married Mark and that he can go screw himself.

She wrote:

Jack:

I don't know why I'm writing to you. I guess I just wanted you to know that I am over you and have married Mark. He has been an angel for me in helping me get over what you did to me, and I will be indebted to him the rest of my life. I have finished the coursework for my masters and plan to finish my dissertation this summer or this fall. Mark finished his last summer and is in the PHD program for history now at McGill University in Canada, where he went to avoid the draft. Jack, I try not to hate you, but it is hard. Nothing has ever come close to hurting me like you did, and as I wrote earlier, I will never forgive you.

Do not write me back. I do not want to hear from you. I just wanted you to know that I am married now and happy again. My life is good, and I don't miss you at all. Not anymore.

Melanie

Chapter Thirteen
The Taiwan Straits

February 1969

They pulled out of Subic and headed north, Jack sitting in the captain's chair on the bridge and Liam McNamara navigating. It was a dark day, and a steady rain slashed at the starboard-side of the small ship as it approached the Taiwan Straits a day later. Jack drank Navy coffee and smoked Marlboro cigarettes, staring out at the waves that seemed to grow by the hour. T. P. Burwell was OOD, and all of the bridge personnel wore foul-weather gear. The waves came out of the east, from the vast expanses of the Pacific, which was where typhoons—called hurricanes in the Atlantic—originated before sweeping into the Philippines and Taiwan and Okinawa. The wind was directly off the starboard-side, and it was increasing. The Black rolled hard but plowed ahead.

Jack had ordered them to pipe in Armed Forces Radio out of Saigon throughout the ship during working hours, and it blared onto the bridge now with the Fifth Dimension and 'Age of Aquarius' and John Fogerty and the Credence Clearwater Revival singing about proud Mary and a bad moon rising. The sailors loved it, and they danced through the day. But Jack's mind was not on the music now. It was on the weather, and he was deeply concerned. Maybe there was a bad moon rising in the Black's path.

Jack told Burwell to have the Boatswains Mate page Liam McNamara to call the bridge. Within a minute Jack's phone squawked, and he picked it up. "Liam, what do you think is going on with the weather? It seems to be getting worse by the hour. We're rolling like a sonofabitch—probably close to thirty degrees each way and taking green water on the bridge. You got any idea what's going on?"

"No sir, Captain. I didn't see this coming. There's a storm coming west off the Pacific with high straight-line winds but the Notice to Mariners said it was going to pass to the south of us. The only thing I can figure is that it turned north and is hitting us now. I'll check and see if anything has come in to revise the earlier forecast."

Within minutes, the sound-powered phone screeched. Jack took it.

"Captain, I've just received a new NTM and it reports that the storm has turned north and I've plotted where it is. I think we're right in the middle of it."

"Can we turn back, Liam, and dodge it?"

"No sir. And we can't go forward and outrun it. The storm is going to hit us broadside in a matter of minutes with straight-line winds up around a hundred miles per hour."

"Holy Toledo, Liam. Jesus. Well, there's nothing we can do about it now except ride it out."

"I'm afraid it's going to push us toward mainland China, Captain."

"How far are we from the mainland?"

"Thirty miles. We're right in the middle of the straits."

"Do you know how much of this water they claim as territorial waters?"

"I don't but I can find out. Give me a few minutes."

McNamara went below.

"Mr. Burwell, have the crew set condition zebra. I want this ship buttoned up and battened down like an army tank. And no one topside except the watch."

"Aye sir."

The keening wind increased until it was shrieking through the bridge. The windshields were covered with water that the ancient wipers strained futilely to disperse, and the Black tottered from side to side worse than Hinky Henderson leading the ill-fated Tacloban Death March.

Liam McNamara returned. "Captain, China claims territorial waters out twenty nautical miles. We're about ten miles out."

"Okay, Liam. Hinky, come right to zero nine zero. Let's get our bow into the wind and see if we can put some distance between us and the chinks. Put some turns on. Go all ahead flank."

"Aye, Captain." He turned her into the wind, and she began pitching. Green water splashed on the bridge, thirty feet above the sea. The waves swallowed the ship up as she struggled against the wind, pounding her as her bow rose out of the water and then crashed on the other side of the wave, so that the next wave swept over the top of the ship.

Jack went below to ensure that the crew had battened down and was ready for the storm. The Black's bow rode over the waves then slammed into the troughs. She shuddered with each slam as her stern came out of the water with her twin screws spinning. Except for the men on watch, Jack ordered the entire crew into their racks. He returned to the bridge about thirty minutes later.

And then came a call from Bob Tyson. T. P. Burwell took it. "T. P., tell the CO that we're losing power on the port engine. I don't know why but she's going down. Tell him she'll be completely down in a couple of minutes."

"Okay, Bob, but stay on the line. I'm sure he'll want to talk to you."

Burwell reported the disaster to Jack, who said, "Oh my god." Jack took the phone.

"Do you have any idea what's going on, Bob?"

"No sir. And I won't until we get into the engine, which means we are going to have to virtually take it apart to figure it out."

"How much time, Bob?"

"An hour or so to get her broken down. I don't know how long it'll take us to repair it because I don't know what's broken. Another hour to get her put back together and get the engine online. I think we are looking at three hours. Minimum."

"Very well. Go on and get started. Keep me posted. And Bob, what speed do you think we can make on one engine?"

"Six knots top."

"Jesus. We're going to lose ground rapidly. Okay, get to it."

"T. P., put your rudders hard to starboard to offset loss of the port engine and let's see if we can maintain some semblance of course. I'll contact Paul and get a message off."

He told Paul Sessums to send another message to Comseventhfleet and Comphibron Eleven giving them the Black's position and telling them what had happened with the engine and that they were being pushed by the storm toward Communist Chinese waters.

It now became a waiting game, and time was not on the Black's side.

Jack sat in the captain's chair watching the sea try to eat the Black. "How are we doing, Liam? Are we making progress?"

"No, sir. We are losing ground. The storm is pushing us west and pretty fast. We've lost two miles in the last half-hour. That's four miles an hour. If it takes the snipes three hours to repair the engine and this wind holds, we're going to be two miles inside Chinese territorial waters when they get the engine back on line."

"Tell Mr. Tyson to go balls to the wall getting this thing fixed. Tell him we don't have three hours. T. P., get Paul up here. I want to send a message and let the staff know our situation."

"Aye, sir."

He wrote to the staff in Yokosuka with a copy to Commander Seventh Fleet, gave them his position and said, "Ship is now eight miles from Chicom territorial waters. Winds around one hundred knots. Course zero nine zero. Losing ground rapidly against wind and sea. Will enter Chicom waters in two hours if cannot complete repairs sooner."

"Send it flash, top secret, Paul. I don't know what they or anybody can do in this mess. We'll just keep fighting and see if we get a lull and can push east away from the mainland."

They were shouting now, trying to be heard against the howling wind. "Skipper," T.P. Burwell shouted. "Mr. Tyson says he's going as fast as he can."

"Very well. Maintain course and speed, Mr. Burwell."

The Black fought on, the small shallow-draft, high-profile ship riding high over wave after wave, then shuddering when she hit before ploughing into the next one. The men called it 'stumping', but she had never stumped like this. Below decks, seasickness was endemic. The men threw up into any container they could find, and those who couldn't find a container retched on the deck.

The waves ripped the forty-millimeter gun on the bow loose and tossed it into the sea. "God almighty," Jack said. "This is some bad shit. How're we doing Liam on headway?"

"Captain, we're losing ground rapidly. We've lost twelve-hundred yards in the last twelve minutes. We're losing a hundred yards a minute." Three miles an hour.

"How far are we off the closest Chicom land mass?"

"A little more than twenty-five miles. At this rate, we'll be well into their waters in another two hours."

"Jesus. Well, we'll just have to hope that they don't find us in this weather."

"I'm saying my prayers, Captain. I just hope the big admiral in the sky is listening."

Jack stood on the wing of the bridge and watched the ship fight against the wind and sea, which continued to come at them in mountainous waves that slammed into the little ship and pushed her back, back toward Chinese waters. Maybe, just maybe the sea was too rough for the Chinese to send anyone out. Maybe, just maybe they would not pick the Black up on their radar. Maybe Tyson would get the engine back online early. Maybe.

"T. P., check with Bob and see how they are coming."

Burwell rang Engineering. "Are you making any progress, Bob?"

"No, T. P. We're working as fast as we can but we can't find the problem with this damn thing. We're taking her apart and that's slow work. We're just about there but not quite. And once we get the engine broken down, it's gonna take some time to figure out for sure what's wrong and repair it. How we're doing up there?"

"Not too good. The storm is pushing us toward the Chinese land mass. We're gonna be in their territorial waters pretty soon if you don't get that engine back online. The storm may save us but we don't know whether they'll send anything out or not. Keep us posted."

Three minutes later the sound-powered phone screeched again. Burwell took it. He listened, then he said, "Captain, they just told me that they're fairly certain it's a problem with the air compressor and they're just about there in breaking her down but not quite. If that's what it is, we'll have to replace it. That's gonna take another two hours then putting her back together will be another hour so four hours total."

Liam McNamara, still navigating, said, "I think it's fairly certain we're gonna enter Chinese waters. We're only twenty-two miles out and they haven't even gotten the engine broken down yet so they can start repairs. Maybe we'll get a break in the storm and be able to get out of here at six knots but unless we do, we're gonna be in their waters pretty quick."

"Well, Liam, tell CIC to be on the lookout for anything coming out from land. The weather's too bad for planes. If they come out, it'll be surface vessels."

Time passed, and the Black passed, too: into Chinese waters. Then it happened.

The sound-powered phone operator reported it. "Sir, CIC has picked up six contacts bearing three-one-five degrees, twenty point six miles on a course of one-three-five degrees at a relative speed of twenty-two knots. They'll be on us in less than an hour."

"Very well. Looks like we're gonna have to fight 'em. We'll wait until they're a little closer to go to general quarters. No need to keep our people sitting there doing nothing for that long. Ortiz, pass the word on the sound-powered phone that we'll be going to GQ in about thirty minutes."

"Aye, sir."

"Liam, this is exactly what we didn't want. But we got it. In spades. The truth is, though, that they're gonna have the same problem shooting at us as we do at them in this storm. I suspect since it's six of them, they're sending gunboats out. If it were destroyers, they'd probably send just one or two."

Then, with the contacts about twenty minutes out, Jack called general quarters. He ordered them to man the two fifty-caliber machine guns on the bridge but not the remaining forty-millimeter on the stern. It was too dangerous to put anyone on the main deck. Hinky Henderson and his crew manned the five-inch gun by the hardest, as the Black continued to take waves and shudder when she slammed into the troughs. The rocket crews took their stations on the eight rocket launchers, though there would be nothing for them to do.

On the bridge, they looked to the northwest with their binoculars. T.P. saw them first. "Okay, Captain," Burwell said. "I got a visual on them. They're small. Probably gunboats, and they're coming on hard. In these seas, I don't know what they're gonna do but it looks like we're gonna find out."

Jack watched as the column formation of boats moved into a line formation—all six side-by-side and pounding through the seas. The Chinese boats then spread out and moved into a circle around the Black. They used their engines to maintain their positions.

Suddenly men appeared on deck manning their deck gun, which looked like a three-inch naval rifle. Their guns then swung around toward the Black, but mercifully, the sea remained too rough to fire. The men on the gunboats waited. On the Black, they, too, waited.

"They're going to stay with us until this storm abates and then they'll probably demand our surrender," Jack said. "And if we don't surrender, they'll open up with all they got. And if they penetrate those sand bags then we're on the road to glory land."

"Captain, I hate to say it," Liam said, "but looking east it looks like I can see light. This damn sonofabitchin storm may be passing."

"Liam, tell the five-inch mount to pick one out and lock it on and be ready to fire when the sea settles. Get the stern forty millimeter manned and ready to fire at anything in his arc of fire. Tell Hinky and the five-inch guys to hit one and then to move to the next one and keep doing that. We'll try to get as many of them as we can. T. P., tell your fifty-caliber guys to be ready. We're gonna need everything we've got to fight these bastards off."

"Aye, Captain."

"And ask Bob how they're coming down below. Even if we do get the engine back, we can't outrun them. It will let us maneuver some, though."

T. P. rang Engineering. Then, "Bob's on his way up here, Captain."

He appeared, grease-stained and haggard. "Captain, we've got her broken down and it's the compressor, which we need to replace. Replacement is going to take two hours. Minimum." He paused to let this bit of information sink in.

Then: "Captain, I may have a shortcut. I may be able to jury rig the compressor. The problem is that if it doesn't work, we've wasted an hour. Do you want me to try?"

"Yes, go ahead. Another hour isn't going to matter. And if you can do it, we can get some power to maneuver and at least make it tougher for them."

The storm gradually passed. The seas calmed. The Black began to move forward, to the east. The gunboats moved with her, maintaining the circle. One of the gunboats hoisted an international signal: "Heave to. We are coming aboard."

"That's what I figured. They want another Pueblo. They want to capture us and use us for propaganda."

"What're you gonna do, Captain?" Liam McNamara asked.

"We're not going to let them board, I can tell you that much. We're gonna do what I said Bucher should have done with the Pueblo: fight 'em."

"Aye, sir," Liam said, smiling as he remembered the wardroom conversation.

"Tell the mounts to be ready to fire on a moment's notice. We'll let the Chicoms make the first move."

"Ortiz, tell the signal bridge to reply negative. T. P., tell Main Comm to get out a flash to Comphibron Eleven and Comseventhfleet that we're surrounded by Chicom gunboats. Give T.P. our position, Liam, and T. P., request air cover."

"Aye, sir."

Liam said, "With this low ceiling and cloud cover, it's gonna be difficult for planes to come in here and do much."

"Well, request it anyway. The clouds may lift by the time they get here."

The Black was making about five knots now, headed east, when the first shot came. It hit about thirty yards in front of the Black and exploded when it hit the water.

"Keep going, T.P."

"Captain, signalman reports a new signal. They're saying, 'Heave to or we open fire'."

"*Will* open fire? Hell, they *just did* open fire. All right. Ignore it. Tell Hinky to lock on to that boat and stand by."

Then it came. A storm of bullets from their large machine guns that slammed into the bridge and pilot house. Jack shouted: "Tell Mister Henderson to open fire, Ortiz."

And Mr. Henderson did. The problem was that the mount still couldn't hit a moving target. It was underway training all over again, and the five-inch crew fired high and low and right and left of the target. The old fire control system was pathetic.

Like Indians circling a wagon train in a 'B' grade western movie, the gunboats moved around the Black, firing their heavy machine guns into the superstructure. It was clear that they did not intend to sink her, only force her surrender.

The bullets tore into the steel surrounding the bridge, chewing it up. It was Hue all over again. Ortiz, the sound-powered phone operator, was the first to go down. His head exploded. The bridge began to disappear. The roof over the forward part of the bridge was blown away, and the metal bulkheads, about five feet high, resembled a bad car wreck.

Liam McNamara and T. P. Burwell were killed almost simultaneously, T.P. with a gaping, sucking chest wound and Liam McNamara with the back of his head blown off. The bridge's radar exploded. Its gyro compasses on each side were shattered, and Jack went below to the pilot house, which was more heavily fortified and where the watch could close heavy steel hatches and slotted combat covers over the windows. He would drive the ship from there.

What greeted him at the bottom of the ladder from the bridge horrified him. The pilot house crew had opened the hatches when the storm passed and had failed to relock them. Both the helmsman and the lee helmsman, who communicated with the engine room, were dead. The boatswain's mate of the watch lay upon the deck, gurgling. He had taken a shot to his neck. Jack slammed the hatches shut and took the wheel and put on the lee helmsman's sound-powered phone. "Engineering, this is the captain. What is your status?"

"It's the captain, Mr. Tyson," the sound-powered phone operator said. "You want to take it?"

Tyson came online.

"How are you coming with the engine?" Jack asked.

"I think what I suggested is going to work. We're putting it back together so I'll know for sure in a few minutes."

"Very well. Everyone up here is either dead or badly wounded. I'm in the pilot house, steering. I'm going to make a one eighty and head for the mist that's following the storm. Let me know when you can come online."

Jack turned the wheel hard to port and began executing a one-eighty-degree turn. The fire from the six gunboats tore into the Black. The large-caliber machine-gun slugs that the gunboats sent penetrated her sides but lodged in the sandbags, so that the rocket crews were safe. Henderson fired on with the five-inch gun, with just enough accuracy to keep the gunboats at bay. When Jack squared her up on two seven zero, dead west toward the Chinese mainland and toward the squall, the forty mike-mike on the Black's stern opened up. Then Jack felt a surge, and his sound-powered phone crackled. It was Tyson. "We're back online, Captain."

"Great, Bob! Give me everything you've got."

The gunboats stuck with her, raking her with machine-gun fire, as the North Koreans had done with the Pueblo, trying to force the Black's surrender. Up ahead was the trailing squall, nothing like the storm they had gone through but with enough cloud cover that it would allow the Black to disappear into the mist. Jack steered her on. Tyson gave him power for twelve knots. The five-inch gun and the stern forty millimeter kept the gunboats at bay. The Black slipped into the squall. The gunboats did not follow. They would wait until the squall passed and then attack again or, if the Black did not come out, follow her until she ran aground on the Chinese coast.

Jack called CIC. "Wallis, get some men and go topside and knock down the posts and the lifeline and take the pins out of the rockets. On the double!"

"Aye sir. What are you gonna do, Captain?"

"Those sonsabitches may sink us but we're going to go down fighting. I'm going to use the rockets on those bastards."

Wallis and a dozen men raced to the deck. Down came the lifeline and posts, and the locking pins came out of the rocket launchers. It took seven minutes. Wallis reported back, "Captain Stockwell would be proud of you, Wallis. Great job!"

"Thank you, XO."

"All right, Wallis. I want launchers one and five level and three and seven down five degrees. Same on the other side. Two and six level and four and eight down five. I want the launchers aimed directly out to the side, zero nine zero relative to our course, just like the cannons on a sailing ship."

"Aye sir."

"I'm turning this baby around and I'm gonna steer her right through the middle of the pack. When I give you the word, I want every launcher we have to open up with mark nines and proximity fuses and keep firing until I tell you to quit. Get the launchers standing by with the mark nines."

"Aye sir."

"And tell Crowley to get up here on the double and raise the combat ensign. We're damn sure gonna need all the luck she can bring us today."

"And one more thing: put 'Stars and Stripes Forever' on the 1A and broadcast it throughout the ship. We're going to give them everything we've got, including music."

"Aye, sir. 'Stars and Stripes Forever' coming up."

The mainmast had survived the gunboat onslaught, and the large flag broke free of it and went taut in the wind that was blowing the squall to the west toward China. The ship came alive with Stars and Stripes, and the Black prepared for the battle of her life.

Two minutes later, Wallis reported that the launchers were standing by with nine-inch proximity-fused rockets with the launchers aimed out at zero nine zero relative to the ship's bow. Jack called CIC. "Give me a course right into the pack of them."

"Zero eight five, Captain."

"Very well. Here we go. Feed me constant course adjustments to aim me right into the pack of them. You got it?"

"Aye, sir. Zero eight five to start."

Jack threw the wheel over hard to starboard and came around to zero eight five. To Engineering, he shouted, "Pour it on, Bob. Here we go!"

"Course, CIC?" Jack asked.

"Zero eight five still good, Captain. Their boats are stationary."

Jack peered ahead through the porthole, the glass blown out and open to the rain. Jack could see nothing beyond the bow of the Black. Then there was sunlight and then the gunboats, milling about in close formation. Jack steered the Black toward the middle of them.

On the gunboats the crews had relaxed, knowing that their commanders would give them notice when the old scow tried to come out of the squall. Then, one of the gunboat commanders shouted "stations!" The men raced to man their guns. They strained to see into the squall. They could see nothing. Undoubtedly, their commanders had picked something up on radar, because no one could see anything.

Then, there appeared in the fog the spectral outline of a ship that looked like an old Japanese coastal freighter. And suddenly, the fine mist that trailed the squall seemed to part, and through the opening came the ship whose outline they had seen. The Black came on toward them, seemingly unafraid, undaunted by the devastating fire she had taken earlier, undeterred by what awaited her in the bright afternoon sunlight. The gunboats, their commanders thinking that the Black was going to ram them, began to pull away, out of her path, but not far. They knew that her only operable gun was on her stern, so they would stay on her sides and blast away at her superstructure. The five-inch mount was out now. Hinky Henderson and all of the crew had taken a three-inch shell, which had exploded in the mount. They were dead.

The Black powered on, her launchers lowered, her launcher crews ready. The gunboats now opened up with their three-inch guns, aimed high to avoid sinking their putative captive. The shots tore into the Black's superstructure. They would teach her a lesson with their heavy stuff. They would make her surrender.

But she came on.

One of their three-inch rounds tore through the pilot house and out the other side. Machine-gun fire penetrated the steel bulkheads and came through the portholes. Jack took a large slug in his left arm. Shrapnel flew throughout the pilot house. Jack's left arm went numb. He looked down. The hit had taken away most of the flesh above the elbow. He could steer with only his right arm now. Blood gushed from his left arm. A piece of shrapnel grazed his face. More slashed at his chest. He took another slug or bullet or bullet fragment in his right leg, just above the knee. Jack steered her on. Into the sound-powered phone he shouted: "Standby Wallis, here we go."

The Black roared into the middle of the gunboats, splitting them, four on one side, two on the other. "Okay, Wallis. Let 'em have it and don't stop firing until I say so. Fire!"

"Aye, sir. All launchers, fire!"

The nines came out of the launchers so big that Jack could see them. They came at a rate of one rocket per launcher every four seconds, 120 rounds per minute from the Black. The rockets went high, and they went low, and they went at the Chinese gunboats fast and hard. With the proximity fuses, they exploded whenever they got close to a target. And they got close. Very close. Some were direct hits. The level launchers blasted into the pilot houses of the gunboats. The lowered launchers tore into their sides. It all happened so quickly that the gunboat commanders had no time to react. They had underestimated the old ship, and they would pay for it. In spades. The Black roared on, firing. Firing. Firing. And then she was through them, and the gunboats still afloat were engulfed in fire, and their explosions rolled across the water to the Black.

"Cease fire, Wallis. We got 'em."

Jack heard a cheer from CIC. "Wallis, go to the gun deck and tell them to secure and come topside. I want them to see what they've done."

The hatches opened, and up came the gun crews. They pointed and screamed and laughed madly. Then they turned toward the bridge and cheered and thrust their fists into the air.

It was over. The USS Black River had survived. She would not be another Pueblo.

Jack steered on. "Bowden, get a helmsman and a lee helmsman up here to take over. And tell Mr. Sessums to come up here and take the con. I'm shot up pretty bad. Tell the corpsman to get up here, too. Everyone else up here is either dead or dying. I need some help. And tell Mister Duvall to get a camera and take some pictures of this thing. I don't think anybody is going to believe it when we tell 'em. I'm going to circle them one more time so he can get some pictures of what we just did. It's amazing."

Then the helmsman arrived and took over the wheel. Paul Sessums came into the pilot house. "Jesus, Captain. You steered her? How'd you know how to do that?"

"I learned, Paul. Did it at night. Loved it. Found it relaxing. Came in handy today, didn't it?"

"God, Captain. You're shot to shit. Corpsman's on the way."

The corpsman was a first class with twenty-two years' experience, but there was little he could do with Jack's arm. He pulled the flesh together and stitched it and then bandaged it to hold it in place and, with help, got Jack below.

The carnage topside was staggering. In the end, Jack was the only survivor above the CIC level. Liam McNamara, Hinky Henderson and T. P. Burwell were dead. Dave Duvall in Main Comm, Bob Tyson below in engineering and Paul Sessums in CIC were the surviving officers besides Jack, and Jack was blown to hell.

Air cover arrived, but too late. A helicopter from Kaohsiung in Taiwan came out and took Jack and the other wounded in to a hospital. Paul Sessums took command and drove the Black toward Keelung on Taiwan's west coast.

Jack almost lost his left arm. A surgeon named Jimmy Cross from Folsom, Alabama pulled the flesh back together and sewed it and said that it might hold, and it might not. Disease, he said, was the real worry. They would just have to wait and see. Even if he kept his arm, Jack would have only limited use of it. They had to cut away a big chunk of his leg, where a lump of shrapnel had turned his flesh into ground beef. Jack would spend the next five months in various hospitals and rehab centers waiting for his arm and his leg to heal and his wounds to close up. He had to learn how to walk again, how to use his arm again. It was slow, but it happened. In a strange twist, a fellow southerner had saved Jack's arm and leg.

The Navy discharged Jack in September, but prior to discharge he received orders to report to the Old Navy Yard in Washington. He drove east in his green MGB. From the Old Navy Yard, he went to the White House and listened while President Nixon read the citation. Then the President hung the medal around Jack's neck, and Jack put on his cover and saluted Nixon as the crowd applauded. He had received the Medal of Honor.

The incident engendered a firestorm of publicity in a country hungry for a hero, for good news out of a bad war. The AP and the UPI couldn't get enough of the story: how a small, old rocket ship designed for firing at stationary targets ashore had taken on six fast Chinese gunboats at sea and sunk them all. The three television networks sent reporters to the Naval Hospital in San Diego to interview Jack. Reporters visited the Black River in Yokosuka, where she had been towed, and they marveled at the damage she had sustained and had survived to fight on. She would be retired, but they would not scrap the little ship that could. Instead, they towed her to San Diego and moored her there permanently, still a commissioned U. S. Navy vessel, albeit unrepaired. They left her just as she was that March Day in 1969 when she, against all odds, took on and beat six Chinese gunboats. The Navy opened her for tours, a monument to the men who had fought in her and died on her.

Jack went home with a functioning arm and a gimpy leg. His military career was over.

Chapter Fourteen
Melanie

August 15, 1969

It was August 15, 1969. Melanie and Mark walked down a dirt road toward the large field, which held a stage. They had met in Albany, New York. Mark had come down from Montreal. "Jesus," he said. "I had expected forty to fifty thousand. But this? Damn!"

"Me, too," Melanie said. "But it looks like we got that many already here and many more coming. I've never seen anything like it."

They carried sleeping bags and a backpack full of food and another filled with bottles of wine and a small sack of marijuana. The festival, in a dairy farmer's field, was to run three days—from August 15 to the 18th. It would become known as Woodstock.

The smell of marijuana came from a light haze over the field near the bandstand. Mark and Melanie moved in as close as they could get and settled in. It was Friday, August 15. The concert started that evening and lasted until noon Monday. Melanie and Mark stayed for the duration, along with almost 450,000 others. Evening came. The show started.

Early Saturday morning Joan Baez came on, and she sang 'We Shall Overcome', and Melanie wept. The song rekindled her love for the movement. 1968 had been a disaster. They had lost Martin Luther King in April of '68 and Robert Kennedy in June. Eugene McCarthy was the only anti-war candidate left in the race, and she and Mark supported him. The Democratic Party Convention in Chicago had been a holocaust for those who went and tried to protest the war. America seemed to be coming apart at the seams.

Melanie wrote her former roommate, Susan Crawford, now living in Washington:

Dear Susan:

Mark and I went to the most amazing concert near Woodstock, New York. We just got back. It was incredible. They are saying that it drew over 400,000 people. All of the performers except Bob Dylan were there. He is still recovering from his motorcycle wreck. The first day was Friday, August 15, and the concert started in the late afternoon and ran on into Saturday morning. Arlo Guthrie and Joan Baez were the big names we heard early Saturday morning. The second day we heard the Grateful Dead, who were fabulous, the Credence Clearwater Revival, Janis Joplin, Sly and the Family Stone and the Jefferson Airplane. The third day we loved Blood, Sweat and Tears and Jimmy Hendrix was the last act. It took us forever to get out of there, but it was worth every minute of it. Mark, who is my historian, thinks it will go down in history as the greatest concert of all time.

The sights and sounds there were amazing. People had sex out in the open, skinny-dipped in a pond right behind the stage, and smoked pot and used LSD, also right out in the open. Mark and I mostly drank wine, and he smoked a little pot. We slept in sleeping bags. Restroom facilities were nonexistent. We went in the woods. Thank god we took toilet paper. And a lot of us went topless. Betty Friedan would have been proud, I loved it. So liberating.

I hope you are well. Write when you get a chance.

Love,
Melanie

Chapter Fifteen
Chapel Hill

October 1969

He had left there almost two years before, and some of it had changed. As he drove through the town in his old green MGB, an anti-war demonstration—a sit-in—simmered in front of the army recruiting building, and the participants chanted their mantra: "Hell no, we won't go." The male students wore bell-bottomed jeans and Beatle haircuts, the females full flowing skirts with wide belts and oversized peasant blouses. Their hair was long now and straight, a far cry from the bouffant hairdos that Carolina girls had worn when he had been there before.

The town, physically, however, was unchanged. The pungent smell of burning leaves hung heavy in the air, and an early autumn chill gripped the place. The leaves had turned red and gold and burnt orange, and the sky was a Carolina blue. Equable buckskin-colored grass covered the sidewalk-laced quad, and the old white cupola stood silently in the autumn sunlight, the sun's rays canted now, so that its light strained to penetrate the myriad old-growth trees that stood serried against the soft blue sky. All of it engendered a feeling of sadness in Jack, He had a sense of gloom with the season, which he had loved before Vietnam, but now it was a season of death and dying, portending the darkness of winter to come. Jack had seen enough of death and dying. Autumn was no longer a joyful time for him.

Jack wore his Ole Miss school clothes: khakis, a button-down light blue Gant shirt, Weejuns and navy-blue gold cup socks. He wore a navy-blue crew neck sweater against the chill, and he stopped at Smitty's, a hoary meat-and-three, for lunch. They let him borrow their Chapel Hill telephone directory, and he found the entry: Mark Goldberg on Old Chapel Hill Road. After lunch, he headed that way. He did not call first. He did not want to take the chance that she would tell him not to come.

Melanie came to the door when he rang the doorbell. Jack barely recognized her. She wore the new de rigueur hippie look, and her long hair was parted in the middle and partly obscured her face. But there she was, and there he was, and the last two years melted away. "God," was all she said.

"Hello, Melanie."

"I don't know whether to slap you or hug you." She looked at him up and down, and then said, "After what you've been through, I think I'll hug you. I have to remind myself that what you did to me is all in the past now and we can't change it, can we?" Then she wrapped her arms around his neck and held him in a cool, polite embrace. She said, "Jack, you know that Mark and I are married now, don't you?"

"Yes, you wrote me. Congratulations."

She pushed him away. "Let me look at you again. God, you're thinner. Your face is more angular. Harder looking. And you are so tan, lots more than before. But you've still got those green eyes. What are you doing here? Are you out of the Navy?"

"Yes, I'm out. May I come in?"

"Yes. Sure. As I think I told you, Mark's in Canada. The draft ran him off. He got his notice and bailed out. I finally got my masters dissertation done and got the degree this fall. I'm done for now but he's working on his PHD up there. I met him in Albany in August and we went to the big concert at Woodstock. I will go to see him in Montreal at Christmas. He likes it up there but most of all he likes not going to Vietnam."

Jack looked about the semi-dark house, suffused with the strong, sweet smell of marijuana and incense. On the wall, there were large posters of rock and folk music icons: Joan Baez, Bob Dylan, Jim Morrison, and Joe Cocker. James Dean smoked a cigarette, and his ghost haunted the living room from a wall. A poster of the Beatles on the cover of 'Sergeant Pepper's Lonely Hearts Club Band' hung beside him.

"I have a roommate. That's the source of the pot smell. I don't use anymore. Nothing but wine. I had to quit to write my dissertation and I don't intend to start back."

"What're you doing if you're not going to class?" Jack asked.

"I'm waitressing at your old haunt, the Rathskeller, nights. Go on at five and work to closing, twelve or one depending on the crowd. Great tips. Make a lot of money. Pays the rent. How long have you been out of the Navy?"

"I got out in September, right after the ceremony in Washington. It was an early discharge on account of my wounds. Drove home and stayed there awhile and then drove on up here."

"Tell me about your wounds."

"I almost lost my left arm but they managed to save it. I got a good bit of shrapnel all over. Had to do rehab with my arm and my right leg where I took a hunk of shrapnel above my knee and I had to learn to walk again. I almost lost it, too. I'll never run races or lift weights again but I'm pretty much okay now."

"I read about you. You made the papers and the news. TV news. Everyone knows about the Black River and you. You're a hero, aren't you?"

"No. Not really. I just did what I was supposed to do. The heroes are the ones who died over there and those who died fighting to save my ship."

"Well, that's not what we heard on the news. I was and still am proud of you."

"Even though you hate the war?"

"Even though I hate the war. But what you did was not part of the war to me. It was the Chinese and you didn't deserve to be attacked when you were and you had the right to defend yourself and you did a good job of that. Do you have your medal? Is it in your car? I'd like to see it. I saw President Nixon present it to you. It was on television, on the CBS evening news. I've never seen a Medal of Honor. Yours will probably be the only one I ever see."

"No, it's home in Mississippi. They had a parade for me in Concord. I wore my uniform and medals and rode in a convertible and the high school band marched in front playing patriotic marches and 'Anchors Aweigh'. It was really touching but kind of corny. I didn't mind though. Concord is nothing but love and it was good to feel love again after my time overseas."

He hesitated and then spoke again. "Well, I guess I need to talk about the pink elephant in the room. As you know, I had to get married over there. Didn't have any choice. Thought I had gotten the admiral's daughter pregnant. The admiral would have court-martialed me over a jeep I stole at Cam Ranh Bay if I hadn't married her. I don't know whether I did or didn't get her pregnant. She claimed to miscarry a month after we married while I was on the gunline. My personal theory is that she was twenty-eight and the clock was running on getting married and having a baby so she stuck it to me. We got a divorce while I was in the hospital in California. She didn't oppose it. I think that after I was shot to hell, she was glad to be rid of me I was so gimped up. At the time we thought I might lose both my arm and my leg. So, anyway, I hired a lawyer out there. Being mutual it was quick and easy. Everything's easy in California. The women, the sun, the beaches, life in general."

"How do you feel about it, Jack? I mean about the marriage and the divorce."

"Like shit. The marriage is all part of the Vietnam debacle and the whole amorphous mass of it rides on my shoulders like a hundred-pound weight."

They were silent as Melanie digested this information.

Then she cleared her throat and spoke: "Would you like coffee? Tea? A glass of wine? Anything?"

"No, I'm fine. I just wanted to see you, see what you've become, hear what you've done. What you're going to do." He paused. Cleared his throat. Looked out the window into the bright sunshine. "I guess—no, I know—I still love you," he said. "And I know I always will."

"I frankly don't know what I feel about you, Jack. I was so shocked that you did what you did and I was hurt and felt betrayed and I was angry. I'm over most of that now because I understand now what you had to do and what you went through and I'm sorry. But you made the decision to have sex with that woman and you did it while you were engaged to me. It almost killed me then and it still hurts now. I said then that I would never forgive you but I guess now I do, now that you're here and I hear what you've got to say. But I will never forget it."

"Well, like I say, I love you and I always will. But there's nothing we can do about that now. What's done is done."

"Yes, that's right. I'm married to Mark now and I've chosen him and this—academia—for my life. When he finishes his PHD maybe this draft stuff will be past and he can come back to the States and we'll find a school somewhere where he can teach and I'll go back to school and get my PHD and teach, too. It's the kind of life that I've always dreamed of. Only I dreamed of it with you rather than Mark. That didn't work out very well, did it?"

"No, it didn't. And it's my fault, Melanie. And as I wrote you, I should have married you when you came to San Francisco. I was stupid and afraid of the unknown and I blew it. And I blew it when I had sex with Amanda and got into that mess and I learned once again that bad decisions have bad consequences, and in this case a terrible decision had terrible consequences. But all of that's past now and you've moved on and it's time for me to move on, too."

"What're you going to do, Jack?"

"I'm going to start law school at Ole Miss next semester. Until then I plan to take it easy."

"Jack, you've changed. The old sparkle in your eyes is gone. You never smile. You are way, way more serious, almost sad. What's happened to you?"

"I lost all of my joy over there, Melanie. That experience was—how can I say it? —jolting and jarring and sobering. No, I think the correct word is *searing*. Yes, it was *searing*, to say the least. The things I saw and did there are just indescribable and the feelings that they caused will be with me the rest of my life. I think that all the enthusiasm I had for life back before Vietnam is gone. And all of the confidence that I had about my life's path, about where I was going, is gone, too. Gone with you and gone with Vietnam. I just don't feel much of anything anymore. Just emptiness. And sadness. But I did want to see you and tell you that I love you and always will and wish you the best—you deserve it—and tell you goodbye because I doubt that I'll ever see you again, and I wanted to say goodbye in person. And I will have to live with losing you for the rest of my life."

"I'm so sorry, Jack. I really am. And I guess that somewhere in the deep, dark recesses of my mind and heart, I still love you. And I guess I always will."

"Please do, Melanie. I need to feel that you've forgiven me and that you still love me and always will, even if it's just a tiny bit."

"Well, you were an important part of my life, Jack, and I'm sorrier than you'll ever know that it didn't work out. I loved you more than anyone or anything I had ever known. And I wanted to marry you and spend the rest of my life with you. And I guess I still ache with that loss. And I guess I always will."

"Well, I believe this is it, then. I'll go on and let you get ready for work."

"No, don't. Stay and have a glass of wine. I can call them and tell them I'm going to be a few minutes late. It won't matter. They don't care. And there's so much more I want to know about you. And I would like for my roommate to meet you. She's quite taken with the fact that I once went with a guy who won the Medal of Honor."

"I don't think so, Melanie. There's not much more to say. I'm staying with an Ole Miss friend who is doing a residency at the Duke med school hospital and I'll go on over there and see him. Then I'll drive up to Washington and see Navy friends there and on to New York and visit some Concord friends and then to Newport and visit some more Navy friends and then head home. I'm going to move to Oxford when I get back and do some prep work for law school that the dean has given me and sit in on some classes because I'll be competing with people who have already been there a semester. That'll pretty well occupy me until I enter law school in January. I have plenty of money now that I saved up in Vietnam and I get disability pay and will get the GI bill so I can pretty much do what I want. The Ole Miss law school is going to waive tuition because of the medal and my two purple hearts. It should all work out."

"I just wish you'd done this two years ago. I tried..."

Jack held his hand up, palm out in the stop position. "Don't say it. It's done and it's past and, as they say, the past is immutable. I can't change it and I need to move on from it so let me. I screwed up and I blew it and I know it. And I know what I lost. I lost you and so much else but it's over and done with. As Doctor Douglas used to say in historiography, it is what it is. What I did has changed me in a way that my life will never be the same. Never."

He stood. "I guess I'll go on. I've loved seeing you, Melanie, but it's time to go."

She stood and walked over to him and held him tightly against her. He felt her body next to his, and it was as though it was two years ago, and Vietnam had never happened. He wrapped his arms around her, and she kissed his cheek and then pulled away. She was crying.

Through tears she said: "Oh, Jack. I don't want to say goodbye forever. I don't. I can't stand to think that I will never see you again. In spite of my marriage to Mark, I do love you. Still. I have trouble admitting it but I do and I always will. Seeing and being with you brings it all back. Oh god, it hurts so much. But I'm married now and I can't—or won't—act on my feelings for you. I can't *just leave* Mark, can I? Not after he was there for me when you did what you did with that woman. I mean, that wouldn't be right."

"No, I guess not. I made this bed for both of us, and both of us have to sleep in it, just not together."

He kissed her lightly on her forehead and turned and walked to the front door and then turned to her one more time. He opened his mouth to speak but then stopped, as though he had reconsidered. He gave his head a small shake—two almost imperceptible twitches—as if to say no to himself, and after a pause, he opened the front door and stood for a moment looking out at the golden Chapel Hill autumn afternoon. And then he was gone.

Chapter Sixteen
Requiem

October 1984

He sat on the sun porch of the large old house in Concord, Mississippi, where he lived. His mother had remarried in 1975 and moved to Biloxi, and Jack had practiced law in Concord for twelve years and now lived alone in the family home, a large two-story brick structure that looked out over the town. There was no woman in his life. He had never married, although he had dated several women in Jackson until a few years before when, one-by-one, they married, and he had aged out of the dating market. "Besides," he often said, "what woman wants an old man, and hell, I'm old. I'm over forty."

He looked out at the golden Mississippi Indian summer day. It was afternoon. The late day sun was headed south now, so it was low in the southern sky, and waning sunlight limned the polychromatic leaves of the large pecan trees that stippled the front yard on Houston Hill, as the people of Concord knew it. Dying brown leaves drifted aimlessly and silently to the ground, and overhead, songbirds darted furtively from tree to tree as they prepared for their winter journey south. In the old days, he might have been hunting doves on an afternoon like this or, on early autumn mornings, large red fox squirrels in the old-growth timber of the Mississippi Delta. But he was beyond that now. Since Vietnam and the Taiwan Straits, when he had looked death fully in the face, he detested killing anything.

God, how I miss her, he thought. *How could I have blown it like that? I had her and then like a damn fool, I got drunk and screwed Amanda and blew the whole thing apart. And then Melanie married Mark and was gone and it was forever and forever is, as they say, forever, which is a long damn time. So here I sit, all by myself. I haven't tried a case in over four years. The attacks come at random times and take my breath away and make me shake and wrap my arms around myself. My face turns white and my mouth turns to cotton and I lose what little confidence I have left. I don't know what these spells are. What's going on with me? What's wrong with me? And there's no one to ask.*

I can't take the chance of having one of those spells during a trial. I did that once and it was horrible. I just panicked. Wanted to run. Wanted to get out of there. Had to stay and fight through it, though. And thank god it passed and I was able to finish the trial, which, after that performance in front of a jury, I lost. All I can do now is an office practice. Wills, trusts, estates, child custody, uncontested divorces, property transactions, that stuff. And I hate it. Hate it. I'm nothing more than a glorified law clerk.

And I'm tired. Just tired. Tired of practicing that kind of law, tired of living alone, tired of struggling with the memories of that time and that place and all that I saw there, all that I did there, all that I lost there. Tired of feeling bad and being sad and fighting these disabling attacks that roll in on me at unpredictable, random times and overwhelm me, like those waves in the Taiwan Straits. I'm tired of drinking myself to sleep alone every night and waking up the next morning with a hangover and feeling just as bad as I did the day before. I'm just tired. So tired.

He took the Army forty-five pistol that had been his father's during an earlier war and placed the barrel in the same place that Cork had placed his fifteen years before, and he didn't pause to think about what he was doing but just pulled the trigger, and with that explosion, it was over. The long fight, the savage struggle, the gnawing loneliness, the sudden losses of control, of confidence, the memories, all of it was gone.

Jack left instructions. He wanted to be buried in Arlington National Cemetery, to which he was entitled as a Medal of Honor recipient. Paul Sessums, now a lawyer in Washington, made the arrangements. Then, on Halloween Day of 1984, the Navy conducted a funeral service with full military honors at Arlington for James Alston 'Jack' Houston, Medal of Honor recipient. And although his name would not be etched on the Vietnam Memorial wall, he was as much a casualty of that awful war as those whose names filled it.

There was only a small group in attendance, but Melanie was there, as were Jack's mother and sister, but she would not speak to them. There was no reason to do so. Melanie lived in Washington now and worked at the Pentagon, of all places, and had seen the small article about Medal of Honor winner Jack

Houston in the *Washington Post* and how he had taken his own life. She now stood in the shadows of a skeletal black-oak tree and watched. Watched them remove the casket from the hearse, heard the comforting words, listened to a homily in which the minister of St. John's Episcopal Church, Paul Sessums's church, recounted Jack's extraordinary heroism that day in the Taiwan Straits, when he prevented the USS Black River from becoming another Pueblo. And then the bugler played a sad, haunting rendition of Taps, and eight sailors fired three volleys that shattered the deadening silence of that solitary place, and they lowered Jack deep into the welcoming brown soil of northern Virginia.

She had not seen Jack since that October day in 1969 when he had visited her in Chapel Hill. Her marriage to Mark Goldberg had ended in 1974, and she had considered calling Jack in Mississippi and telling him. But she hadn't, because she didn't want to admit to him that she had made a mistake in staying with Mark Goldberg when she probably could have had Jack when he came to see her in 1969. *Besides*, she had thought, *he's probably married with children, and I have no right to jump into his life and interfere with that.* And so, they stayed apart, each wondering about the other, each living solitary lives.

And now, she wondered: *Could I have saved him? Could we have reconnected in '74 when Mark and I split? Could Jack and I have married and come through it together if I had contacted him when Mark and I divorced? Probably. But I didn't give myself and Jack that chance. I screwed it up, just like Jack screwed it up back in '68. And it makes me so sad. So, we each missed the other, sliding past one another like two lost souls, each of us on ships going in the opposite direction, each of us living on the dark side of our lives.*

And I go back to that day he came to see me in '69 and I could have had him then and yes, in retrospect, I could've left Mark at that time. I didn't love Mark in '69 any more than I loved him when we divorced. He was just there when I lost Jack and I turned to him in my sorrow and took him because he was there, which I never should have done and I stayed with him out of some stupid misguided, misplaced sense of loyalty.

Oh God, to think what I missed when Jack came to see me. I could have had him then and saved him, and instead, I lost him forever.

Melanie would grieve what she had lost for the rest of her life, for she had lost heavily, though not as much as Jack who, to his shattering end, mourned all that he lost there: Melanie, his optimism, his joy, the positive trajectory of his life, his confidence that life would get only better, his ability to smile, all of the things that had been his before the savagery of Vietnam.

Oh ghost! Oh lost!
Oh gone! Forever.